STABAT MATER

Tiziano Scarpa

Translated by Shaun Whiteside

D0928526

A complete catalogue record for this book can be obtained
from the British Library on request

The right of Tiziano Scarpa to be identified as the author of this work
has been asserted by him in accordance with the Copyright, Designs
and Patents Act 1988

First published as *Stabat Mater* in 2008 by Giulio Einaudi editore

First published in this English translation in 2011 by Serpent's Tail,
an imprint of Profile Books Ltd
3A Exmouth House
Pine Street
London EC1R 0JH
www.serpentstail.com

ISBN 978 1 84668 769 3
eISBN 978 1 84765 646 9

Designed and typeset by sue@lambledesign.demon.co.uk
Printed in Italy by Legoprint S.p.A., Lavis, Trento

10 9 8 7 6 5 4 3 2 1

Supported by
ARTS COUNCIL
ENGLAND

Lady Mother, it's dead of night, I got up and came here to write to you. Just for a change, anxiety has me in its grip again tonight. It's a beast well known to me now, I know what I must do in order not to succumb. I have become an expert in my own despair.

I am my sickness and my cure.

A tide of bitter thoughts surges up and grabs me by the throat. The important thing is to recognise it straight away and react, without giving it time to take over my mind entirely. The wave grows quickly and covers everything. It's a black and poisonous liquid. The dying fish rise gasping to the surface with their mouths wide open. Here's another one, it comes up with its mouth wide open, dies. That fish is me.

I see myself dying, I watch myself from the shore, my feet already drenched in that black, poisonous liquid.

Another fish in its death throes comes to the surface, it's the thought of my failure, I'm still here, I'm dying again.

Why float to the surface? Better to die underwater. I'm being dragged down. I feel myself sinking. Everything's dark.

Then I'm on the shore again, standing, still me, still alive, I'm looking at the poisonous sea, black to the horizon, swarming with dead fish, their mouths wide open. They're me, we're me, a thousand times over, a thousand dying fish, a thousand thoughts of destruction. I've died a thousand times, I go on dying without ever leaving my death-throes. The sea swells, salty, it's poisonous, black.

I'm the fish with the veiled eyes, the one that has risen to the surface to die. I look up, above my head. There's a pale horizon, the clouds are dark, like an inverted sea, the cloudy sky consists of frozen, blurred waves.

I see the shore of a tiny island, down at the end there's a girl looking around. She's watching me die, she can't do anything for me. That girl is me.

Do something for me, girl on the shore, do something for yourself. Don't let yourself be embittered by what lies within you. Wherever you turn you see your defeat. The black salty tide, it's full of dead fish. React, don't give in.

Have to hurry up before I'm completely overcome, while there's still one small corner of my mind that can see what's happening. I have to drag myself there with all my strength, withdraw into that nook that's still capable of making decisions, and say: I.

I'm not this decay, I can still do it, I'm strong, I don't want to let myself dissolve in this black poison, I'm not all this death that I see, I don't want to swallow this sea, I won't let all this darkness enter me and wipe me out.

I'm still there, somewhere, I'm here, separate from this devastation, anguish hasn't taken all of me yet, there's still a corner where I can take refuge and say: I.

If I can still do it, for tonight I'm safe, I'm capable of getting up and leaving my weary bed and coming here to write to you.

Lady Mother, just for a change, tonight once more I found myself with my eyes wide open staring at the ceiling. It isn't really a ceiling, to tell the truth, because above me there's Maddalena's bed. In here we sleep in rows of beds fixed to the wall like shelves. The ones sleeping in the lower beds have a kind of personal ceiling above their heads, made of the boards of the higher beds.

So my ceiling is the boards of Maddalena's bed. It's quite low, if I raise my arm I can touch it. Of course I don't, because I know myself by now, I'm too absent-minded. But sometimes I've raised my arm while thinking about something else. I touched the boards with the tip of my fingers, unaware that I was doing it, I took a splinter from one corner and then, still lost in thought, I started scratching the wood with my nails.

'What do you want?' Maddalena asked me suddenly, leaning over the edge of her bed, above me, her whole head. It made me start. In the darkness I made out the outline of her tousled hair, it looked as if it was surrounded by black snakes.

'Did you want to say something to me?' she asked. I didn't say a word, I really had nothing to say to her.

Forgive me, I'm telling you things that are of no importance. The wooden splinters on the bed-boards. I'm ashamed, Lady Mother, I beg your forgiveness. But I had to start somewhere, you don't know anything about me, you don't know anything about anything.

When the anguish comes, almost every night, the infallible remedy is not to linger in bed. Then I get up and come here in search of you. Summer and winter. In the winter, particularly, leaving the covers does me good, it wipes out all horrors at a stroke, like a bucket of icy water. It doesn't matter if I feel chilly. My body is used to these cold nights. It's always better than letting yourself be tortured by bad thoughts in that hot, unhealthy bed. I climb the stairs, I come up here and sit on the top step, leaning against this wall, which gives off all the heat I need. It's my secret place. To get here I put on a shawl that protects me, it makes me think of you. Lady Mother, I'm wrapping you up in my thought, do you feel me?

I've raised my arm, I touch the boards of the bed above me, I break off a little splinter, scratch the rough surface, a head leans over the edge, instead of hair it has lots of black snakes.

'What is it, did you want something?'

'Who are you?' I ask.

'I'm your death,' says the head with the snake-hair. It has a nice voice.

'Will you keep me company?' I ask.

'Do you want me to take you with me?'

'If it's all right with you, I'd rather not die quite yet,' I say.

'Then what do you want?' The head goes on talking gently to me, it hasn't lost patience.

'I'd like you to stay with me forever.'

'And what do you want us to talk about?'

'I don't know,' I say.

'I don't say much.'

'That's all right.'

'And besides, there isn't much to say,' says the snake-haired head.

'It's enough that you're near.'

'To do what?'

'I'd like you to help me never to forget you.'

Lady Mother, do you remember me? Do you know my name? Let me introduce myself, I'm Cecilia. Do you like that name? What would you have called me? Did you think of a name when you held me inside you?

('During my brief stay in your belly', I was about to write.)

Yes, I am intimate with darkness, but I'm not at all proud of it. I would happily take my intimacy with darkness and barter it for a few hours of sleep, to restore my spirit and give it a bit of peace. I can't tell you when I developed the habit of getting up at night. But there's one thing I'm sure of: the first memory I have of me, the most long-ago memory, is darkness. It's the truth, I'm not exaggerating, my first memory as a child is my eyes wide in the darkness. You might say that my childhood was nothing but a long sequence of darkness. I'm not saying that to complain, or to hurt you in any way. That's simply how it is.

Lady Mother, have you ever found yourself imagining me? Have you ever wondered how I spent the first years of my life? If you want your imagination to depict the truth, you have to think of a child spending the night with her eyes open, tortured by anguish.

You mustn't think it was the darkness that frightened me. Or the silence. Here there is never complete silence. By day the rooms are full of voices and music. At night you can hear the breathing of the sleeping girls. Each one of them has her own particular way of breathing in her sleep, and when I'm not disturbed by other thoughts I quite like spending the night telling their breathing apart. Some snore, but it doesn't bother me. Each one of them has a nocturnal personality, which sometimes contradicts the personality revealed by the light of day.

Every morning, like flowers, the sun makes the faces bloom.

When she sleeps, Maddalena breathes heavily, resting must be a great effort to her, while by day her step is light, her words are delicate, she likes to smile. Perhaps she has exhausting dreams, in which all the things she has managed to avoid during the day collapse back upon her.

Every now and again, when I have stretched out in my bed in the dark, I catch some indecipherable little creak, in the distance. It seems to be done specifically to remind me that in here we're in a huge, complicated building, full of halls, rooms big and small, and stairs dug like burrows in the hollow spaces between the rooms, and flights of stairs that climb diagonally, suspended above architectural chasms.

I try to imagine the journey that sound has made to reach my ears, coming up the stairs, moving down the corridors, slipping through cracks, passing through locks and doors. Sounds, even the spookiest ones, have always been a comfort to me, because they distract me from my thoughts. Pricking up my ears, staying there listening, I travel far from myself.

Sounds are my outward thoughts. They're the part of my mind that is outside me, beyond my outline, far away from my body. They are my most vast self.

Do you want to know what I think when I'm ill? I couldn't say exactly. I feel lost, completely lost. At those moments I'm sure that there's nothing to be done for me, everything is bitter.

'You mustn't upset yourself so,' the head with the black snakes says.

'What can I do?'

'I don't know.'

'Do you think it would be better for me to die?' I ask.

'Perhaps. Try and imagine yourself dead.'

'How?'

'However you like.'

'I see a still, cold body.'

'But where are you?'

'Outside that body, somewhere, in the air. I'm imagining it.'

'I don't like that. You've just changed places. You have to imagine yourself dead from within.'

'Should I imagine I can no longer imagine myself?'

'That's it.'

'It's impossible.'

'Then leave it, if you can't do it. Go and write to your sweet little mummy, go on.'

'But you... You... !'

I call her again, many times, in a whisper, but the snake-haired head doesn't answer me.

Sometimes, in the dark, I have the impression that I can see something above me, a kind of big spiny ball. It's a craggy sphere completely covered with very long spines, like a hedgehog, but rocky, made of stone. What for me is life, my life, evil.

Lady Mother, I've learned that when it happens to me, and it happens to me every night, I absolutely mustn't stay in bed torturing myself, I have to get up and come here to you.

I creep out of the room, I walk down a very long corridor, I slip into an almost invisible passageway that only I know and climb the little staircase to a landing below a closed door. It's one of the many staircases in the building. I sit down on those steps, at the top. In the winter I lean against the wall, with a stove-pipe passing behind it, warming the bricks. I sit there for a while at the top of the stairs until the anguish passes. Below me I feel the stairs plunging to the centre of the earth. I clutch the banisters so that I don't fall too.

If you knew how tightly I have gripped that cold metal in my hand for all these years! I could mould it with my eyes closed, with clay, remaking it this way and that way, if they asked me to. I know its shape by heart, the little leaves that decorate it, made of iron, quite sharp.

I've just written something stupid. Why on earth would anyone ask me to remake the banister in clay? What good has it done me to know those metal leaves? What good has it done me to learn by heart all the details of the world?

Lady Mother, you must be patient with me, meaningless things come into my mind, but that's how it is in here, things repeat themselves and we become familiar with lots of small details.

Always feeling the same shape of the same metal leaf attached to the banister of the stairs. Always meeting the same broken floor tile, every morning, going from church to the refectory, the first tile in the first corridor on the second floor. Recognising a notch on the brass handle of the door to the hall.

Lady Mother, what an idiot I am. You still don't know anything about me, and I'm wasting my time telling you things of no account. Just think what's occurred to me: I was still very small, it must have been seven or eight years ago. For three days one of my teeth had been wobbling, it was a front tooth, at the top. It was the first milk-tooth

I lost. My companions told me I should get hold of a thread, or make a little braid of three long hairs, pass it around my tooth and knot the other end of the braid to a door-handle, and then slam the door shut. I didn't want to, it sounded too alarming. I pulled out a hair to make the braid, then changed my mind and put it between my lips, sucked it in little by little and bit it to tiny pieces between my teeth.

Then, one night, sitting on these steps, I put my fingers in my pocket, held thumb and forefinger in a pincer shape and gave a tug. One pull and the tooth was in my hand. Its jagged edge glittered in the dark. I was about to throw it beyond the banister, into the stairwell. I bet I would have had to count to a thousand before I heard it hit the bottom, in the centre of the earth. Instead, without thinking about it, I put my little dead tooth back in my mouth and swallowed it. Do you want me to tell you what I felt? For me it was the same as throwing it into the stairwell: something falling, disappearing and being lost in the dark depths. A little piece of me fell inside me and was lost in the void. That night I felt I didn't belong to myself, I wasn't my property, I would never be.

When I was younger my nights always passed the same way. It was as if I was dazed, I sat on the highest step of the flight, on the top floor.

It's the same step that I'm on now. Your eyes get accustomed to the dark, they make do with the little light there is.

So I sat there staring at the corner of the wall, blankly, sometimes for hours at a time. The line where the two walls met looked like a scar to me. The open space, outside, was a wound. Someone must have closed the wound of space by building these walls.

I imagined what was outside, many centuries ago, when there were no walls or houses or anything, when there was just open space, water and the muddy islands covered with scrub. The wind swept across them, the women were scared, they kept each other company at night, the children huddled in their midst.

A glimmer filtered in from somewhere, into the landing at the top of the stairs. There's always a bit of light left somewhere, at night. But it never condenses in the corners, it isn't like a dust-ball, it's a substance that's subtler than air. It's a foundation.

Darkness is only an appearance, the real foundation is light.

I liked to think that I was inventing it, that little light that there was, because even in the deepest darkness I discovered I can close my eyes and imagine the light, and then it's as if my head were lighting up by itself, from within, in secret I can think the light, turn on a light inside me.

I don't remember when it was that I first got out of bed and spent the night at the top of the stairs. If I think about it, there mustn't even have been a first time. I have a feeling it's been going on forever. I've spent all my nights like that, ever since I was very young, ever since I've been here. I would go so far as to see that I wouldn't be who I am if I didn't have my insomnia. It's a part of me, and I wonder if I would go on living without that nocturnal appointment with my nothingness.

Lady Mother, I'm writing to you in the darkness, without the candle lit, without light. My fingers run over the piece of paper on my knees. I dip the pen in the ink, I dunk it in the heart of the night. I find it difficult to make up the words that unroll on the page, perhaps they too are just lumps of darkness. Within these words, every night I come to pay you a visit. You can't see me, but my wide eyes are looking at you.

I've just written that the words unroll, but perhaps they knot themselves. They unroll and they knot themselves, in a single movement. Perhaps I'm freeing myself, or perhaps I'm imprisoning myself.

Lady Mother, perhaps the prisoner is you, knotted in these words. Perhaps I write to you to free you. I vainly wrap this thread around you who aren't there, hoping to catch you. Perhaps this string will form a ball, I will hear a voice muffled within it, calling me to save it, cursing me, pleading to me, asking my forgiveness, accusing me till I bled. It will be you, you will be something, a lump, a rattle, a smile.

'How are you?' the head with the snake-hair asks me.
    'You're back!'
    'I never went away.'
    'It seemed to me that you did.'

'You're the one who doesn't see me. I promised to stay by your side, I've never moved.'

'Really?'

'I keep my word, even though I don't speak much.'

'Are you jealous of me?'

'Why would I be?'

'Did you stay silent because I prefer writing to her?'

'You're doing everything on your own. I didn't protest, I didn't tell you off, I didn't say anything at all.'

'Your silence sounded like a reproach.'

'You really are a girl. I overestimated you. I'm wasting my time, with you.'

Is there anyone less alone than me? I mingle among the other girls. There are hundreds of us, I'm sure that to an outsider's eye we all look the same. And in the middle of them I'm indistinguishable, completely ordinary. I eat with them, I pray with them, I'm taught with them, I play with them. I'm one of them, no more and no less. And yet it is precisely that community living has fortified my solitude, it has made it indestructible.

I'm a red-hot metal plunged into water, my solitude has turned to steel. They tempered me by plunging me into chitchat, into the group, into uninterrupted shared life. I am the invisible one, the solitary one.

Lady Mother, are you there? Do you exist somewhere? Are you still alive? Have you ever been? Am I writing to a ghost?

I'm gradually starting to form an image of you. A plausible image, I mean. Don't think I never dreamt about you during those years. But it's only recently that I've started imagining you as you must really be. At least I think so. Everything I was used to thinking about you was only the consolation of a frightened child, an image of comfort, made to measure to explain my condition.

I was even convinced that you were an evil witch. Seriously, don't laugh. I imagined you as a witch with a big black cloak, you filled the night with chilling laughter, as you deposited a bundle in the Ospedale alcove, that's how I imagined you.

The nuns never told me anything about you. Anyway, that's the rule here. They don't say anything, we don't know whose daughters we are. But I got the idea that in this respect at least the nuns don't hide the truth from us. They don't even know where we come from.

Increasingly often, all of a sudden, I am visited by your face. Usually it happens to me while we're eating: I'm sitting at the refectory table, holding my spoon, I lean slightly forward over the plate and spot the outlines of a head on the surface of the soup, I think I can make out your face. I see you, Lady Mother: you're still a girl, you're having dinner with your parents, before I was born, sixteen years and some months ago. You are leaning over your plate, clutching the spoon as if you want to break it. Your eyes are downcast, you have a lump in your throat, you can't swallow that spoonful, you have to pretend there's nothing wrong, you wish you had a mirror in front of you to check your expression, you're afraid that your face will betray you, and your father and your mother have understood that you're pregnant. But the soup isn't a mirror, the potatoes and the onions float in the middle of your reflected outline.

I have to struggle to imagine you even better, but in those moments I seem to start getting closer to you, to begin to know you.

I try to feel within me the shame that you must have experienced. What does it feel like to bear a mistake within you?

Some days ago I came into the kitchen in the afternoon and stole a little bit of pig's heart. I wrapped it in a little cloth, I hid it under the banister, between the metal and the steps, I left it there to rot. Today I put it down my front. Even through my shirt and my frock you could smell the stench. My companions turned up their noses, looked at me with horror, others laughed. Sister Teresa took me aside and gave me a lecture about personal cleanliness, which is 'the first thing', she said.

What's the first thing? Being honest? Staying a virgin and intact? Loving your own filth? Carrying your own mistakes by your heart? Not abandoning your children? What's the first thing, the most important thing?

I look at Jesus on the cross, he's dirty, he's sweaty and bloody. He has a wound that's leaking blood, like women. He's like me.

Did you yield to love or a whim, poor Lady Mother? Or

perhaps you were attacked by a violent man. Have no illusions, that isn't enough to forgive you, nothing will ever be enough.

'You're treating me like a naïve girl.'

'I'm not treating you at all. I'm here and that's all,' says the snake-hair head.

'You don't scare me, I've learned not to be afraid of anything.'

'So why did you want me near you?'

'To show that I'm not even frightened of my death.'

'You don't know what you're saying. You can't look me in the face, you're writing to your mother to keep me at bay.'

'But I was the one who called you!'

'And do you think I've really answered you?'

Lady Mother, I implore you but you don't reply. You're only in my head, I look at my thoughts coming out of the tip of my pen, I throw them out of my head without ever managing to free myself of you.

Every word that I write is only another way of saying your name, the name I don't know. Even if I write sky, earth,

music, pain, all I'm ever writing is Mamma.

Do you want me to tell you about the time when you didn't exist? I'm not joking. There was a time when I didn't know that mothers existed. Perhaps that was my happiest time. I didn't miss you. How could I have? I didn't even know I had a Mamma.

I remember it well, that night. I don't know how old I was, perhaps four, five. I'd already developed the habit of nestling away up here, at the top of the little steps at the top of the stairs, in the depths of the night. Eventually I noticed that someone was wailing somewhere, in a place far from the building. You could hear a kind of moan from the bottom of the stairs. Who knows, maybe some sort of dying animal. Maybe a rat had been trapped and its belly had been crushed by a spring, it still had an amount of suffering to endure before reaching death. But it wasn't a rat, it wasn't an animal, that was a human voice, a voice that called to me.

I got to my feet and started going down the stairs. All of them, to the last step. I followed that wail, it was just a thread that rose from the bottom of the sleeping building.

I was apprehensive, I was afraid of being discovered by the nuns who took turns keeping an eye on us, at the end of the corridors, sitting on a bench, dazed as they repeated the rosary.

During the night some girls get up, some use the pots in the cupboards in the corridors, others have to use the latrine on the ground floor. The nun who stays awake lets them go one at a time. But this happens on the other side of the building, on the other staircase. I know the darkness by heart and I know how to turn the blind corner of the corridor and reach my favourite staircase without being seen. I am a part of the darkness, a bit of black moving in a bigger black.

I went on going down, further and further, and with every step I took I called myself more and more of an idiot. The stench that came towards me from the bottom of the building was unmistakeable. There was a latrine down there as well. And yet I didn't think I'd ever been there. The wailing was coming from in there.

Lady Mother, I write to you at odd moments, secretly, before I sleep, the little sleep I manage, when I write

I'm completely exhausted, defenceless, when my mind no longer has enough strength even to dream. I look at the words that are coming out from the tip of my pen and spreading wearily over the paper. I sit staring at them like that, quite shattered with the effort. I look at the word Mamma, I go on looking like that, I write it again to understand it, I stretch it out, I pull it in all directions until I tear it, Mamma. I have no other way of looking at you but that.

Peering into a latrine was something I'd never done. Why would I? I have never been curious, not even as a child. I was always busy with my thoughts, I couldn't take an interest in other people, girls, musicians, nuns. But the wail beyond the door of the latrine continued. It was a torn and anguished moan, it expressed a strange ferocity, a voice of pain. There could have been a monster in there. Maybe it had drawn me down there to devour me. Let it, I didn't care, in fact it would be much better that way. So I gently pushed the door, and I looked.

Lady Mother, I haven't written to you today, did you notice? I don't think about you, and you don't exist. My life is a way of not making you exist. Sometimes I find

myself thinking: today I'm not thinking about my mother.
That's how I take my revenge.

A girl was squatting in the latrine, facing the wall. I didn't
recognise her. She had her back to me, and the place was
very dark. Somewhere the moon must have been there,
laughing at me: the girl who thought she had gone down
into the abyss to be devoured by the monster and had
found a girl tormented with colic. The moon is a thing
stuck up there to laugh at women.

In front of me I saw a black figure, an outline contorted
with an intestinal cramp. I had gone all the way down there
to the bottom to stand and look at one of my companions doing her business! What a joke. And how stupid.
A fetid mass was coming out of the bottom of that body,
the girl was panting, she was clenching her teeth, I heard
her imploring the Mother of God. It was disgusting, I was
about to go away, but that thing wouldn't stop coming
out of her guts.

Don't blame me, Lady Mother, never in my life had I ever
spied on a human being while she was doing her business,
and certainly that scene didn't attract me, and yet I stayed

there for a while longer, there was something that kept me down there, I'd never seen such excrement in my life, nor known anyone suffer so much to free themselves of it.

Then something entirely senseless happened, something monstrous and comical at the same time. The excrement started to cry.

Lady Mother, I'm nothing, I don't exist. I could die at this very moment and would be forgotten immediately. There's no one who thinks of me, no one who's fond of me. I'm not complaining about this. On the contrary, sometimes that thought consoles me. I have no responsibility for anyone. I could go mad! Kill one of the nuns. Any of them, for no reason. I would be pardoned and forgiven, I'm sure, they would punish me with impassive cruelty, serenely, as is only right. I would be understood straight away. I am nothing.

How vast, this nothing of mine. I feel myself everywhere, I feel that in that everywhere I don't exist, and that thought goes to my head.

I imagine the water unconfined, beyond the walls, the

muddy islands with the wind stirring the scrub, and I'm not up there, I'm not like the spirit of the Lord God moving on the face of the waters.

I try to imagine how he must feel, the Lord God, being everywhere, but everywhere in the opposite way to my being everywhere too. The Lord God is present in every single tiny detail, while I'm everywhere like the void.

I'm absent from all the places there are in the world. How vast is this absence of mine! When I think of it my head spins. But then I think that this non-existence is just another illusion, and suddenly I'm all here again, inside my skin, I clot, and in fact for some days now one of my nails has grown in, the big toe of my right foot hurts. Perhaps that happened to me precisely because I'm here, always and only here, in my place, inside me, and my presence can't cope anymore, it's pressing and making itself felt, it stings me.

'You never speak.'

'You're the one who isn't calling me,' the snake-haired head replies.

'I'm worried about disturbing you.'

'I'm keeping watch over you, remember that, I'm always here.'

'Should I feel reassured?'

'You're the one who wanted me.'

'There's too much difference between us. Too much of a gap. You're powerful, I don't count at all.'

'There's nothing I can do about it. I'll leave you if you want.'

'No, stay here! But let me make myself useful.'

It seems to me that the snake-haired head smiles at my suggestions, but without any sarcasm. It has its usual gentle expression.

'Make you useful? How?' it asks me.

'Do you want me to kill someone for you? Do you want me to kill a nun?'

'Don't be childish. I'm just your death. Yours and no one else's. Don't digress. Don't allow yourself to distract you.'

'So you don't need me at all?'

'No.'

'I thought you'd like me. That you'd ask me something.'

'You have to be the one who asks and the one who answers.'

'Get out of here! You just know how to look down on me. You're proud.'

Out of the body of the girl squatting in the latrine a snake had come, and it remained attached to the excrement. The snake's tail was still trapped inside the girl's guts, while its head sank its teeth into the belly of the newborn little body. The girl picked up the little body and pulled the snake from its belly with a bite. The snake lay rolled up on the ground, flabby and inert, still dangling from the girl's guts.

I made off up the stairs.

I was four years old when I witnessed that scene, I knew nothing of life. Now I'm nearly sixteen, I know even less.

Only a short time afterwards, in the light of day, I worked out why the girl had invoked the Mother of God. Looking at the altarpiece in the church I saw her, the woman crushing the snake beneath her feet. But even more bravely the Mother of God has defeated the horrible monster that came from her body. She holds him in her arms, defenceless now, a rosy, smiling child, tiny and innocent. The Mother of God has tamed that monster.

After that night I suffered from constipation for months.

How could that girl have concealed her pregnancy? She must have bandaged herself up very tightly over the last months before she gave birth. Such pain, hard to imagine. And the fear of being discovered. Was she really a girl? What if she had been one of the nuns? I don't know. Many years have passed since then. At least eleven, I think. I was very young, I must have been four, five at the most, the night when I witnessed, without knowing it, that childbirth in the latrine, and then it was dark, the woman had turned her back to me. I don't even know what happened to the newborn boy who was brought into the world that night. Or was it a girl? It could even have been one of our companions. She would be eleven years old now, unless she died in there, the poor creature. But if the newborn girl was found alive, the nuns will doubtless have covered up the scandal. Nothing easier, for them, to pretend to have found her in the alcove of the Ospedale from some stranger, one more, one less… I vaguely remember that in the days that followed baptisms were celebrated to welcome the new little arrivals. But that had always been the standard policy at the Ospedale. Perhaps I should examine my companions' faces more carefully. Or the faces of the younger nuns: why not? Them too, the sisters too. Who's to tell me that it wasn't one of them who had got pregnant? I should confront the faces of all the little girls of about ten and the women of over twenty-five, to see if I can see any resemblance, some family connection between mother and daughter, perhaps... Lady Mother! As I was writing these words I shivered, I thought that the same thing could have happened to you, to me and to you. And what if it was you in there too? If you'd given birth to me in there as well? Maybe you live here, among the hundreds of women and girls who live in the Ospedale, and you look at me every day, and at night you secretly watch over me, you're sleepless too, you're huddled up somewhere in here waiting for me to come and visit you by writing to you, I who think you're who knows where, without knowing that in fact you live in here and now you're somewhere here nea

Yesterday I stopped writing to you and wept.

I'm angry with you. I'm not going to write to you anymore.

'You're just making a fool of yourself.'

I don't say anything. I don't answer the snake-haired head.

'Why don't you answer me?'

'I don't feel like talking to you,' I say.

'Come on, I'm the one who isn't expected to speak. When I open my mouth, you have to see it as an honour that I'm doing it to you, a real and genuine gift.'

'Your head's got swollen.'

'Have you gone mad?' She said it with one of her kind laughs. What drives me out of my mind is that the head of black snakes never changes, it always addresses me in a very gentle voice.

'You would be nothing without me. Without me my death wouldn't exist, you wouldn't exist either,' I say.

'We're giving ourselves airs, from what I can see. Fine, I'll keep my trap shut, it must mean you don't…'

'Forgive me. Say the same to me, please.'

'Oh, that's easy. You're denying the evidence. You've got it into your head that your mother might be somewhere in here.'

'Do you think that's impossible?'

'I think it's fairly unlikely.'

'But that isn't to say that…'

'Think what you like. But the only one close to you here at the Ospedale is me. Until you understand that, you'll be going around in circles.'

We all dress the same. A grey dress for every day, tied at the throat. We wear a red dress when we're singing in church. The uniform is supposed to make us indistinguishable, and instead it produces the opposite effect, it only emphasises the differences between one face and another.

We're left with only our faces to express ourselves with. My companions' personalities are concentrated entirely in that little surface, the oval of the face. When they talk to me, I can hardly look them in the face, I feel as if I were being slapped, so violent is their constrained expressiveness. Their faces seem to have been carved from within. Those muscles, trained to modesty, barely move beneath the skin, but all the shock force of those imperceptible spasms reaches me, so dense is the concentration of character that surfaces on their faces.

I wear a face of stone, I don't show myself. I pass unobserved.

Lady Mother, I want to tell you a dream that I have had many times, with eyes open, sitting on the stairs, during the night. There was an old woman, with a black skirt and an enormous belly. The woman was wandering around a dark city at night. She crouched down and did her business in a hole full of excrement. Then she stood up again, tidied herself, her skirt was covered with perfumed flowers, her belly was slender, her face smooth, she was beautiful and young. She walked away from there without wanting to. On the pyramid of faeces there were two eyes, the dirty face of a baby, me.

Tomorrow will be my birthday, I will be turning sixteen. Tomorrow, the twenty-first of April. You're surprised, Lady Mother? You didn't remember that was my birthday, did you? But that's the night you left me in the Ospedale alcove, so that's the date the nuns put in the register. For them, I came into the world that night. And I agree, I approve of their diligent impartiality.

The day of my true birth, in this world, happened towards the inside, when I was brought into the Ospedale. You didn't give birth to me by making me come out of your body, but by slipping me into this building.

Lady Mother, years ago I dreamed that I was wandering
at night along the streets of a strange city, with a sharp
pain in my belly. I knocked on doors, asking for shelter
at all the houses, but all the doors were opened by evil
old women with yellow eyes and rotten teeth. I couldn't
shake off the weight pressing down on my guts. At last,
filled with shame, in front of a group of boatmen who
watched me with a sneer, I squatted down and did my
business on the ground, right where I was, in the street.
The boatmen exploded with laughter, their mouths, ringed
with black hair, opened up, their teeth sparkled. I turned
to look and saw that in the midst of my excrement there
was a pair of eyes, a filth-smeared face, two little hands.
The newborn child was me. I walked away, starting to
sing softly, towards the group of dark-bearded boatmen.
When I woke up my thighs were wet, I had had my first
blood.

Lady Mother, I'm trying to imagine you as best I can, I
want to burst through this blindness, this empty place,
this face that I miss. I'm putting my all into it. I imagine
the day when you discovered you were encumbered with
me. A while ago, in the refectory, I lowered my head onto
the plate served to us by our companions in the kitchen.

The silhouette of my head was vaguely reflected on the surface of the soup, a face made of onions and cabbages. I imagined you, you too bent over your plate of soup, hiding in your heart your shame, me. You were absurdly trying to guess from the reflection of the soup if your distress was leaking from your face. But you could see only onions and cabbages. A repugnant vapour rose from your reflection.

Lady Mother, you appear to me increasingly often when I'm sitting at the refectory table, I see your silhouette in the soup, I get up and run to vomit in the latrines.

Lady Mother, it's always you that I turn to, in spite of my plans and my impatience, I always turn to you, always with the same words, I always tell you the same things, because you're always the same thought, you're my repetition, my litany, my sentence, my tedium.

Lady Mother, I'm describing you as I see you when I try to imagine you. I'm telling you how you were in the dreams in which I've met you. But I realise that it hasn't yet occurred to me to tell you what I'm like. The fact is that I don't know. I don't look at myself in the mirror. Here at the Ospedale there aren't many mirrors. Our vanity certainly isn't encouraged by the nuns, but neither is it entirely mortified. We have to remain within bounds. That's what the only big mirror in the great hall of the Ospedale is for. We are allowed a few moments to check that we're neat and tidy. So in the mirror, even if I want to, I don't see myself, I see the law of this place applied to me.

The law is a girl in a grey tunic, narrow, taut lips, she looks into the depths of my eyes in the mirror, she puts a nail in my gaze, she hurts me.

Yesterday was my birthday. At breakfast the nuns recited a prayer for me. Then silence fell in the refectory. Maddalena sang a song that I had never heard before. One at a time, and then in groups, my companions followed her, weaving their voices in with that tune with ingenious counter-melodies. It was a present for me, a little chorus composed on my name. How strange it is to hear your own name being sung! The music was so sweet that, as I listened, I felt rather proud to hear myself named in such a melodious way. But then I worked out that this sensation of bliss had nothing to do with my name, it was entirely due to the music, and my name, the word that I am, could not sustain all that beauty, it was no match for the music. The hundred voices that sang my name, murmuring it so affectionately, without meaning to, were tearing it to pieces, reducing it to scraps by filling it with music, as if they were slipping the sun into a sock.

'I need you.'

'I'm here,' replies the snake-haired head. I'm starting to sense something mechanical in her monotonous kindness.

'You think you've noticed a false note in my voice, don't you?' it says.

'Can you read my mind?' I ask, startled.

'Of course. Are you surprised?'

'No, you're right. I wanted to ask you something.'

'Tell me.'

'Did you ever have a Mamma?'

'You're asking me if your death had a mother as well?'

'Yes.'

'That isn't a difficult question.'

'Then answer it,' I say to her.

'I have the same mother as you.'

'So we're sisters.'

'Twins, I'd say.'

'And she abandoned you, too?'

'Why do you want to know?'

'It would hurt me to know that she left you as well.'

'Would you want your mother to take care of your death?'

'Yes.'

'She did that by bringing you into the world.'

So it was that, more than ten years ago, I learned how we come into the world, believing that the woman in labour was doing her business. Lady Mother, you can imagine my thoughts after that night, when I went into a latrine, when I in turn felt the stirrings of a bowel movement. After I had evacuated myself, I didn't have the courage to turn and look at what had come out of me. I didn't have the courage to turn around, and yet I didn't leave the latrine straight away, I stayed and waited in there for a little while, in silence, to hear if a voice behind me didn't start bawling.

Lady Mother, before that night I didn't even know that mothers existed. I spent the first years of my life without the thought of you, without the spectre of you. Can you imagine it, a world without mothers, you who no longer exist for me, who have never been, who will be forever?

One day a little girl approached the fire, in secret, to look at her face for the first time, on the surface of the water in the pot. She wanted to discover her secret, the secret of herself that was known to everyone but herself. The little girl leaned over the pot to see her face reflected on the surface of the water and know the truth at last, but the reflection was quite broken, the water was turbulent, tiny luminous spheres formed in the depths of the pot, they grew larger and larger, they made themselves big and impetuous, they pushed at one another to get out, women's bellies swell, women can't control themselves, they burst.

As a little girl I took what they said about us seriously, that we're all children of the Lord God, I looked around and I saw my companions, the little ones and the big ones, I saw the nuns, I was convinced that He had made us all, with His very own hands, and when a new one was finished He left her straight away in the alcove of the Ospedale, as soon as a baby was ready.

One day, years ago, we were playing in the courtyard,

when the glass door opened and a lady appeared. She was
with Sister Amelia, a young nun, who had recently arrived
at the Ospedale. Our companion was called Anastasia, I
remember, I can't forget, I will never forget. Sister Amelia
was holding a little necklace, from which there hung a
coin that had been cut in half.

'Come here, darling,' the strange lady said to our
companion.

We all followed Anastasia, five or six little girls.

The lady drew a bracelet from a sleeve, from which
there hung a half-coin like the one Sister Amelia was
holding in her hand.

We got a close look at the two halves fitting perfectly,
the head in relief on the coin coming back together, and
the two fragments of writing that surrounded it, ANAS
and TASIA, being reunited, that name shone whole once
more, like a halo around the head carved on that medal.

'Mamma!' our companion said, throwing herself
around the lady's neck.

We never saw Anastasia again, or Sister Amelia who,
I learned later, had been severely told off for allowing a
reunion to happen before the eyes of some girls at the
Ospedale. And for allowing a reunion to take place in

front of my eyes.

After that time I worked out how it was that some little girls disappeared and were never seen again at the Ospedale, even though they weren't ill. There were also the ones who were taken away when they fell sick, often they didn't come back, they were buried far from our sight. But some others left the Ospedale because their mother, their salvation, had come to get them.

Many of us are abandoned in the alcove at the Ospedale with a token on us. They are little medals cut in half, or coins with holy images, broken in such a way that there are no doubts about the person who turns up to claim her daughter, bringing the half of the token that perfectly matches the one kept in the archive registries.

Lady Mother, did you do the same thing? Did you leave a token in the alcove at the Ospedale when you abandoned me that night? It's all I need to know. It would mean that you had a plan to come and get me. Sixteen years have passed by now, you aren't going to come back, I have no illusions about that, if I could see with my own eyes that you left me here with a token, I would know that you at least intended to leave a possibility open. It doesn't matter if you left then, it doesn't matter if you didn't come and get me like Anastasia's mother. It would mean, though, that you decided to go on thinking of me as a daughter, your daughter, in spite of everything, and you would still allow me to entertain the thought of you as my mother, to think of you as a mother.

A broken whole, divided in the middle. Two incomplete pieces. Each leaning towards the part it misses, feeling its lack, desiring it, hating it.

Perhaps the reason I curse you is that you gave me the instruments to curse you with. Do you understand, Lady Mother? Think about it. Maybe if I'd lived close to you I would have hated you anyway, perhaps even more than I find myself hating you here. But with one fundamental difference: I don't think that at your house, whether palace or shack, I would have received the education I have had here. At your house I don't think you'd even have taught me to read and write. Be cursed, you have allowed my curse to take shape.

'You're an ungrateful girl.'

'What have I done to you?'

'You'd rather be a fly, a grain of dust. You'd rather never have been born.'

'Why are you telling me that?'

'Tell the truth.'

'I'm not sure I know what I want. But perhaps you're right, I'd rather not be aware of being what I am. I'd rather not realise that I don't know what I want to be.'

'Listen to your circumlocutions, you've been racking your brains. You're enfolding yourself in your whine.'

'Are you happy with what you are?'

'Me?'

'Yes, you.'

'So, let's hear it, what am I like?'

'As I see you. Your head is full of horrible black snakes that won't stop twisting, they're biting each other, their poisoned tongues commingle, they're kissing one another. Is that how you wanted it, or was it forced on you? Who gave you this shape, who pummelled you into this torment?'

I thought the only one born of a woman was the baby Jesus. I looked at him on the altarpiece, in the arms of that radiant woman. That's why, I used to say to myself, Jesus is called the blessed fruit of the womb of that woman. The Mother of God had the gift to make a baby come out of her body, while from our flawed bellies we imperfect women spew out ugliness and putrescence.

I've also learned the main difference from the painting above the altar, with all those monstrous babies, each one with a pair of wings stuck on its back. Between its thighs it had another imperfection, a defect that was smaller but no less bizarre. From each of them, from first to last, there dangled a fat, nailless finger. Like the wings, I thought this too was a privilege of these exceptional beings. How men are made I discovered from the sex of angels.

The only man I saw from close up for years was Don Giulio. It makes me laugh to think that he too was made in the same way as the cherubs on the altarpiece. I imagine him with that flabby finger hanging between his legs, and the tufted wings, like the wings of chickens to be made into soup, half-plucked, flapping along with the others around the Mother of God. Who knows if there is such a thing as old angels, when they're always depicted as young?

As a little girl I didn't even know what 'man' meant. The

only man for me was Don Giulio, an old man in a cassock, a skirt like our dresses, like the ones the nuns wear, his face not much uglier, and not even that much hairier than the faces of the oldest nuns. His voice, too, croaked like the voices of the older nuns, he was already old when I became his pupil. Don Giulio writes everything we play – the choruses for the masses, the concertos, the motets. Since I was born I've played hardly anything but his music. For a long time, for me, music has coincided with Don Giulio, music was Don Giulio and nothing else, I didn't even know that music written by other people existed, the music was all enclosed within that old body that hobbled around the Ospedale, and eventually it came out; it filled the scores, the rooms, the church, our bodies.

When Don Giulio comes with a new score and gives it to us to copy our parts, I know already what will be in them, I know him so well by now. He's a part of me.

'So are you a part of me?'

'What do you think?' the snake-haired head replies with a question. 'I know, you never reply with a question. But yours wasn't a very clever one.'

'So why didn't I have you beside me? All I had to do

was break a splinter off from under Maddalena's bed and you arrived.'

The snake-haired head falls silent for a moment. 'They say it's something that comes with age.'

'I don't understand.'

'It's at your age that you start thinking about your own death.'

'Really?'

'And the deaths of others.'

'How do you know that?'

'From the way you look at your older companions and the nuns.'

'What do I do?'

'When they speak to you, you look at the black teeth in their mouths, ruined by all the words they've had to say in their lives. And also you don't stare into their eyes, but a bit lower down, you're obsessed by their thick, dark glasses, weighed down by all the things they've had to look at since they've been in the world.'

Lady Mother, don't tell me off for writing on these pages. They're the only ones I can get hold of in here. There's no blank paper, it's too precious, it's reserved for the covers of the scores for the instrumentalists and singers, so I keep for myself the one covered with crossings-out and mistakes, I collect old sheets, torn by accident during the rehearsals, pieces of paper that would otherwise have been thrown away. I have to make do with writing in the gaps on these old scores, in the white spaces. Don't take offence, it's not for lack of respect that I dedicate this space to you. Look at these sheets, full of music and words: they're like my days. The time isn't mine, my time doesn't belong to me. Since I was born I've had to do what they tell me to in here, so the things close to my heart I have to put in the spaces left, in the gaps left empty by chance. I think about you where I can, when I can, between one thing and the other, but you mustn't believe you're of secondary importance to me. Wherever there's room, you occupy it, you're like the air.

Lady Mother, if I'm writing to you inside the stave this once, it's because I can't find any other pages for you, but perhaps also because these words are the melody of my thought as it sings to you. They go straight on, always on the same line, but they are not a monotonous note. When I can write to you in the line occupied by the words of the Kyrie, or the Halleluiah, you could sing my phrases in chorus, like a psalm, or solo, like the recitative of a motet, with harpsichord accompaniment. But these are only fantasies, they are images I have invented as a justification. The truth is that I should be braver and steal the white paper, but I'm afraid of being caught, and then perhaps I endanger these corners of used paper as well. The nuns would discover that I go and write to you at night and they would confiscate everything. They're quite understanding, the nuns, but I don't think they would be happy if they found out that I'm writing to you, they'd disapprove of me keeping a correspondence with my mother. They might get it into their heads that I know where you are, that I've found out from someone, or that I'm trying to trace you and contact you secretly so that I can pass these letters to you. But are these really letters? They seem to me like a hug leaning against the window of an empty courtyard, they are kicks and blows delivered blindly, in the air, in solitude.

I wrote a stupid thing the other evening, when I told you you had to imagine these words being sung. In fact you should imagine the opposite, without music, without a voice, these words are the sounds that ruin the music, disturb it, they cue the rain that pelted down today as we were rehearsing in the hall.

The air has grown dark and has started to blow through the rooms, beating at the windows.

Sometimes I wonder what Don Giulio must think of us. What is it that has made him come here every day for years, teaching the littlest ones how to hold a violin, how to keep the intonation of the voice, etcetera. What do we mean for him? Does he feel sorry for us? Does he love us? Does he see the difference between one and the other or think of us all as particles of a single whole, the ants in an anthill? Are we only an instrument for his music? I don't think so: Don Giulio no longer cares about music now, he's constantly writing the same thing, has done for years now, always the same mass, the same motet, the same melodies, whatever the solemn occasion. He's tired, he's old, he repeats himself.

We instrumentalists are almost all young, we put our young blood into this decrepit music. When we are playing Don Giulio's music, I feel as if I'm wearing the dry skin of a flayed old saint, I fill it with my solid, fresh body. The frayed woman's skin swells, dilates, rips. The music tears itself when we play.

Today Don Giulio protested because we raced as we were
rehearsing a Kyrie. 'Too impetuous! It isn't the Halleluiah,'
he stammered in his little voice. He didn't even have the
strength to shout. You can't work out who has the upper
hand, between his music and us. His music forces us to be
old. It takes us over and slows us down, it rusts us.

'I've been thinking that it's almost too comfortable having
you beside me.'

    'Do you want me to go away?' says the snake-haired
head, with its irritating kindness.

    'Stop getting so angry all the time.'

    'I don't think I've ever got annoyed with you.'

    'I just wanted to tell you that you aren't the most
terrible presence that a person can have beside them.'

    'Are you thinking of offending me?'

    'I'm just saying there's something much worse than
you.'

    'Let's hear it.'

    'Old age. Illness.'

    'Do you want to look your old age, your illness, your
humiliation in the eye? Do you want me to summon them
here instead of me?'

'I just wanted to point out that they're harder to face than you are.'

'Why did you feel the need to tell me?'

'Just because you have a tendency to lord it.'

'Ah, so that's it.'

'Are you cross now?'

'Never in a million years. I'm used to being insulted by everybody.'

It's music written for people who no longer have the strength to do anything. Perhaps that's why he gives it to us to play, since we're prisoners of the Ospedale. What's the difference between the oldest nuns and us? We're always closed up in here, everyone, young and old, girls and nuns. Some nuns have at least chosen it, it's their life. But us girls? Don Giulio writes this worn-out music to make us understand, to make us hear strettos within the rhythms of his concertos, to spur us to react, to find an escape route.

Why are we born? Why did you give birth to me, Lady Mother? I'm wondering whether it wasn't my decision to come into the world. I know, if you put it like that it sounds proud. And yet I see all this old age, this melancholy around me, I see these women, deeply alone, giving each other courage, living in community, I see the nuns talking about death and life after death, about the happiness of souls, but when they talk about it their faces don't light up. We're born to escape a body that is destined to die. Something within us realises that it's destined to be extinguished forever, and then it reacts, it flees.

Children are the fear of dying as it flees our mortal bodies.

The Ospedale is a womb of death, we girls live next to sterile women, the ones who chose to keep within their bellies their fear of death, to keep it whole. We aren't yet born.

Making your own fear of dying die along with you. That's what the nuns do. So I don't know whether to see them as cowards or as saints.

Children spring from their mothers' bellies and burst out crying, still terrified by what they've abandoned, the death they've escaped. They're body-parts of the mother who flees from them.

Mothers try to keep them bound to themselves, they hold them back when they are born, but the babies escape anyway, so the disappointed mothers take their revenge, they incite death against them, the rope that holds them back becomes the snake that bites their little belly and injects it with deadly poison. They too are marked, they were inoculated with their fate in the womb. The snake is pulled away, but in the middle of their bodies children bear a mother-scar, a death-scar, forever.

The woman depicted on the altarpiece has managed to pull from herself her fear of dying by listening to a secret. The angel has bent over her and whispered something in her ear, he has confided in her an idea that came from the Lord God.

The Mother of God pulled from her body the part that doesn't die, which is why we venerate her.

Or else Don Giulio sees us as instruments of his prayer. We are just the violins and the voices that raise Don Giulio's supplication to God. Are musicians privileged in the face of the Lord? Will He receive the sounds that reach Him with greater delight than a poor man's croaky prayer?

But I'm not entirely sure that music rises, that it ascends. I believe that music falls. We play from above, suspended, on the balconies beside the two walls of the church, a few metres from the earth, because music weighs, it falls down. We pour it over the heads of the people who come to listen to us. We submerge them, we suffocate them with our music.

Don Giulio writes music from a life, he no longer has ideas, he no longer has inspiration. He's the brother of one of the governors of the Ospedale, it's the only reason why every year they renew his contract as a violin teacher and master composer in here. How can inspiration be reduced to habit? You just have to glance at the scores to understand that Don Giulio can't do it anymore. He writes out of inertia. Perhaps he's asking God to let him die. He composes these listless short-range concertos, which when we play them don't even rise as far as the church ceiling, they fall back heavily, from the musical balconies where we sit and play them, they plunge down, and the thud that they make as they crash to the ground is Don Giulio's true music, it's his prayer to the Lord God.

'Lord God, look how weary I am, hear how weak my prayer, even though I and my musician girls have climbed up here to aid the ascent, even though we come up onto the balcony to play, my music doesn't even have the strength to touch the ceiling of the church and caress the fresco with you in it and your saints and your Lady Mother, our advocate near you, I no longer have the strength to knock *in excelsis* at the gates of heaven, and yet I have at my disposal choirs of pure voices, the stout arms of young instrumentalists, and instead, all this apparatus serves only to make all the more obvious the flabbiness of my music, of my prayer.'

At the end of a life in which he has composed music *ad majorem Dei gloriam*, Don Giulio must have understood that the glory of God does not increase, we just make ourselves smaller, demonstrate our own inadequacy. Don Giulio is humiliating himself with his second-rate, inadequate, weary music: in the face of God he reveals himself for what he is, a weak man, poor and old. We should offer to the Lord God only our imperfect works, the worst of our fruits.

The church is a big square hall, a musical cube. On the

side walls, a few metres up, there are two big balconies, facing one another. They are a dozen metres long and protrude a few metres from the wall. You reach them by an internal door, on the second floor of the Ospedale.

The balustrade surrounding the two balconies is in two sections: the lower section is stone, the upper one of gilded metal, consists of a lace of openwork ornaments. So the musicians who play on one balcony can see the ones facing them on the balcony on the other side of the church, they can follow their movements and fall in line with Don Giulio's movements as he keeps the beat. But the ones sitting in the pews looking up at us from below can't make out our faces, because the weaves of metal surrounding the two balconies are too dense to the eye as it rises diagonally. For those looking from down there, sitting on the pews, we are a silhouette, an outline. We are a shadow, an imagination, a dream.

We are an apparition that secretes music. We are ghosts exhaling an impalpable substance. We are beautiful because we are mysterious, and we spill beauty into the air, the lie of the music masks our affliction.

Today the church was packed. We came out onto the balconies suspended in the air, behind the grilles. We arranged ourselves on our stools. During the service, at the Kyrie, I deliberately played three wrong notes, very shrilly. I thought about Don Giulio, about imperfect works to be offered to God. I followed the score he wrote for us violins, making it even more perfect in its imperfection, I enhanced the virtue of the melody by multiplying its defects. My little solo became the scratch of a nail on the smooth stone, I was as carried away as I have ever been since I have played, for the first time I felt that somewhere the Lord God was listening to me. I was praying like that with my violin, thanks to Don Giulio's disastrous music, painfully written and yet more painfully played by me, I made it powerful in its weakness with my tuneless playing. I tortured that tune, all too frayed already, I took it to its conclusion by rendering it entirely inconclusive.

As I played I understood that those notes contained a death rattle. Don Giulio had written his own death throes, he anticipated them by imagining what the moments of his death will be like. He had captured the undignified moments of a body crumbling as it shows itself to God for what it is. With my bow I snatched that sound from within Don Giulio's poor scribbles, and I brought it out, I amplified it, I played my surrender, I called my mother, I asked for help with the strings of the violin. I played the powerless creature that is no match for the one supreme moment granted him to live, I played death, I played death out of tune. I felt myself being dragged by the scruff of the neck.

I realised that my companions had stopped playing too and an icy silence had fallen on the church. Don Giulio, conducting us from a corner of the balcony, wore a shocked grimace. I was dragged inside the door that links the balcony to the internal corridor of the Ospedale, I fainted.

'Sleep, Cecilia. Learn to sleep without dreaming. I will comb my snakes and braid them and wrap them on the top of my head, I will not weary you with my discourses, I will not terrorise you with my black face, I will turn to show you my smooth nape, I will make silence around you, I will lay claim to nothing because one day you will give me everything, I will give you a foretaste of the peace that belongs to you.'

Lady Mother, I'm coming back to visit you after a week of rest. I have been treated well and kindly, they brought my food to my bed, I have been spoon-fed, so I haven't had to fear seeing you in the repugnant reflection in the soup. Don Giulio came to ask me how I was, he asked me what got into my head to play, at the mass. I didn't have to confess. 'What the devil possessed you?' he asked me. In my heart I absolved him.

They brought us to take a breath of air. They made us get into a dozen boats, the instrumentalists and the singers, arranged in a little fleet. The boatmen silently pushed the oars, standing in the stern, behind our backs, and yet I could feel the tension, you could guess that they were excited to have us on board, we are strange beings, they think of us as creatures of another world. We went masked because the citizens must not see our faces. I completed the closure of my face by keeping my eyelids lowered too. I preferred to listen to the city. Sounds I had never heard reached me, I tried to imagine what could possibly be producing them.

I keep my eyes closed, I listen. A tool that I have never seen, on one side. I try to imagine its shape, what it's for, how you hold it. On the other side, an animal that I've never met.

I prick up my ears at a sound and envelop it with my imagination, I surround it with a mass, a body, a face, a purpose.

The sound that comes from things is like their purpose, it's their will that goes beyond them and makes them bigger, expands in the air.

The banks ran on either side of the boat, I kept my eyes closed, I heard scraps of conversation and trivial comments as we passed. Then the horizon opened up, we must have been in the middle of deserted water, among the islands, I heard a bell in the distance, it sounded as if they were mending it with hammer blows, that bell was wailing with the pain they inflicted on it.

I tried to distinguish every single swallow above my head by the cries that it emitted as it crossed the sky from one corner to the other, then listened to them all together, at the same time I tried to follow all their courses through space.

There are voices that correspond to the configuration of the body, but there are also bodies that have nothing to do with the voices that flow from them. They seem to be inhabited by someone else. Antonia is a tall, gaunt girl, and she has a bass voice, you really have to hear the dark boom that comes out of that bag of bones. They make her sing the parts that would normally belong to a masculine register. She says it's her father's voice, that her father came to live inside her voice after he died. If I understood correctly, she was the daughter of a sailor who fell in battle near one of our Greek islands.

Sister Teresa stopped me after dinner, she's worried about me, because I don't eat. 'You have to feed yourself, you have to be healthy.' I wasn't punished for the wrong notes. They forgave me, saying it was a blackout, that it's normal for such a thing to happen to me if I don't eat as I should. 'You mustn't refuse food, it's your duty to be strong.'

Lady Mother, I receive the dish on the refectory table and see your reflected outline, I swallow my soup all the way to the end. Then I run to the latrine and throw it all up. I can't keep you inside me.

I confessed, but I didn't betray you. I didn't talk about you to the priest who comes to listen to our sins. Are you my sin?

The priest speaks to us through the grille of the confessional. We can't see his face, nor can he see us. The people who come to listen to us in church, when we play and sing, can't see our faces either, because we stay behind the grilles of the balustrade, high up, suspended a few metres from the ground. They hear sounds and voices, they know they come from the bodies of young women. There will certainly be some who let run their fantasies, down there, imagining us hot, sweaty, tense with the effort of playing and with the fear of making mistakes, our complexions suffused with blood.

I have been troubled by the thought of how we are to imagine the men who come to listen to us in church. By feeling myself inside me, by having a concrete sense of my body, I am reduced to imagining that others imagine me. I can take possession of me only if I think that someone else is thinking of me.

They have never seen us, the musicians are forbidden

to show themselves, and besides, it wouldn't even be possible from behind the grilles. So many of them, indeed, come here to imagine.

We are pure sound, the voice detached from the body.

We are their dreams.

Does it exist somewhere, pure sound, unattached to the instrument that produces it? The sound that frees itself from the string, the voice that isn't confined by the throat that spreads it into the air? The sound and the voice flying, free, without coming from anywhere?

Look at this violin that I play every day, the wood that it's made of, the twisted guts of its strings, the dry intestines. I imagine secretly musical trees, sonorous sap, and animal guts run through with an unheard harmony, in the darkness of their deepest blood.

We were in the courtyard, we heard mewing. Behind a plant we found the cat, the one that usually wanders about here, and which had disappeared a while ago. It was lying on one side, with its eyes half-closed. It raised

its back leg, looking at us. Beside its belly it had five tiny
pink mice.

'It's had kittens,' Rosanna said.

I was very surprised. 'Then it's a female,' I thought, but
I didn't have the courage to say it out loud so that I
wouldn't look stupid for having only just figured it out.
Sister Francesca arrived, she laid a sheet out on the
ground, she took the little ones and set them down on
the white material, one next to the other. The cat watched
her, exhausted from having given birth.

Those little living sausages had their eyes closed, the
skin of their bodies almost transparent, some veins just
visible running beneath the epidermis. The little internal
shadings were moving organs, as if their whole bodies
were stuffed with eyes that might open and blossom in
the light.

Sister Francesca took the four corners of the material,
she pulled up the little sheet, tied it in a bow, walked
across the courtyard and plunged it into the barrel full of
water, under the drainpipe. My companions and I felt a

pain in our hearts. Instinctively I gripped the nun's wrist, I tried to pull the bundle from her hands. We fought, I tried with all my might to save the kittens, putting my head under the water, I thought I could hear the cries of the little creatures. Then a force pulled me away, back, my companions pulling me by my belt. I spat, coughed, was bent double, I had drunk the water of their death throes, I had inhaled it.

'Go and dry yourself, fool,' the nun said. 'Before the Ospedale existed, newborn babies that no one wanted suffered the same fate. You would have found yourselves drowned in a canal, you too.'

Being born without coming into the light.

Staying in your mother's darkness to end up straight away in that of death, passing from the warmth of her dark blood to black, icy water. Not knowing anything of the world, just the warmth of the guts and the cold of the city.

I am feverish. I'm trembling.

Maddalena has leaned over the edge of the bed. 'There are

thousands of them, they say, at the bottom of the canals, tied to a stone so they won't come back to the surface. By now they've all melted away, they've blended with the oozy bottom.'

Every month they take us on a boat trip to let us float on the water of the canals, where the bodies of the little drowned orphans were buried in the centuries before the Ospedale was founded. Our pre-born twins. The blind alleys of life. The boat runs over that cemetery of water and mud. The bodies have dissolved, there is no sign of acknowledgement of them, no medal cut in half, no holy images. Nor are there crosses or stones, no name, the word that we are, that sounds in vain. Our lives float on the dead water.

I dreamed I couldn't walk. Everything was dense and dark. Around me I saw little. Glows, luminescences, scraps of light fog. They flowed towards me, growing clearer as they got bigger. They were babies who had just been born, with disproportionately large heads. They looked at me with the orbs of their huge eyes that protruded behind transparent lids. Their gazes were opaque, phosphorescent, blind. They crowded around me, they pressed me, like jelly-fish, luminous fish. They bumped gently against me, nudging me softly in my sides and on my back. I discovered that I too could float as they did. I understood that I was one of them. They were my chill twins. We swam into the belly of the black mother. Conceived by Lady Death, no sooner were they born than they were dead. I felt a pain below my nape, on my neck, like a bite, I was sucked back up again. A boatman had dragged me from the water with the grip of his strong hand, he looked at me with his black eyes, the same colour as his beard, his face was hairy, infested with maleness.

We play under water.

We play in the belly of the mother, in the guts of death.

We are abyssal fish, we sing our never having come into the world.

Music spreads in the black water. The men and women of the city walk on the shores, they pass in their boats. We are the sirens singing from the depths of the turbid water, no one listens to our black song.

'Maybe you're starting to understand,' says the snake-haired head.

'What?'

'That you belong to me, and not to your mother, or the one you call mother.'

'Isn't her name mother?'

'No.'

'What should I call her? Mamma?'

'Worse than worse!'

'Another name?'

'There is no name.'

'Another word?'

'There is no word.'

'So?'

'She isn't your mother, she isn't your mamma, she's a protection, an excuse not to think about death. An illusion. A consolation. But not even these words are enough.'

'And what about you? What should I call you?'

Lady Mother, I'm treating you badly. Who am I writing to? To you, to myself? I'm not telling you things as one should, because I know you don't exist, and you will never read these letters of mine. So I'm putting down the phrases as they come to me, rather than making myself understood, rather than wanting to make myself understood, as one does with one's loved ones. One flies to the help of one's loved ones with words that make one understood, one writes as if coming to someone's aid. But I don't want to come to your aid, I want to write to you as if you had turned your back on me, to make you see that I ignore you, I despise you, I deposit my excrement with my back to you, I give birth to you. I'm not writing to be understood by you, it doesn't matter to me at all. I'm writing in your presence, parading my indifference towards you, I'm showing you what I'm doing as if you didn't exist, because you don't exist. I'm writing what I feel like, what's going through my head. You no longer exist in my head. I'm constantly writing to you to make you feel how much you don't exist.

Lady Mother, I'm asking your forgiveness, I don't have the right to treat you like this. I know nothing about you. I don't know why you abandoned me here, sixteen years ago. Perhaps you died when I was being born, you died in childbirth and someone brought me here rather than leave me to die beside you, or rather to entrust me to some other family where I would have been considered a lower-rank daughter, they would have treated me as a servant, a slave. Perhaps your husband died in battle, aboard ship, like Antonia's father, while you were pregnant, you have many other children and bringing them all up, on your own, would have been beyond you, you knew that if you'd kept me with you I would have starved to death. Perhaps, perhaps, perhaps. I can only imagine what it was that made you leave me on the doorstep of this Ospedale a few days after I was born. I just know this, the nuns told me that when I arrived here I was very small, I must have just been born, a few days or perhaps even less, just a few hours. That's all I know, I have no idea who you are or who you were, I don't know why I was separated from you.

There are hundreds of us girls here. We are the daughters of young women deceived by men who promised to marry them and who then ran away leaving them in the lurch, or the numerous daughters of widows of soldiers of our republic who died in battle, or there were too many mouths to feed, or…

The other day I talked about it to Sister Teresa, she delivered a speech that I will not easily forget. She said

I mustn't think about it too much, because we're all daughters of God, 'it's the only thing that counts', she said to me, and so far there's nothing strange about that, it's the same old story that I'd heard repeated a thousand times by the other nuns and by the priests in the confessional, in church, during mass, all the time. But the thing the nun told me and which has stayed in my mind is this: 'We all bear within us the corruption of original sin, all of us, from the highest to the lowest, it isn't our birth that distinguishes us before the Lord, because none of us is born innocent. Even the daughters of noblemen are born sinners and are no better than us in the eyes of God, original sin is a blessing, it makes us all equals, the powerful and the wretched, the noble and the disinherited.' That was what Sister Teresa said to me, but she also asked me to keep it to myself.

From an early age they make us sing, they put instruments in our hands to find out if we have any talent. The girls who haven't got a voice or who aren't made for playing are destined for sewing, for cooking, for other trades. The most promising sing and play, and also copy music, they are taught to produce sounds and reproduce them on paper, they learn the harmony of air and ink.

I wish I had the same ability to harmonise words and thoughts, what passes through my head and what I write. I wish I could write with the perfect match that exists between a written note and a played one.

We are musicians and copyists, all of us, we have to know what the music is made of when we fix it on paper and when we make it go into the air. The written notes are like the heads of as many hammered-in nails, we arrive with our musical instruments and slip them out one by one, we pull them out as if we were taking out a nail and freeing it.

Today at mass Father Domenico read us Jesus' words about the lilies of the field and the birds of the air. I've never seen a lily. Birds I've known more from hearing than from seeing, I've never seen them in the fields but I've listened to them flying over the water. Everyone praises the harmony of their voices, but to me they sound very shrill. Indeed, it doesn't seem to me that you can call what they're doing song. The little birds are bewildered by their voices, they're trying to get rid of them.

The nightingale trills to exhaustion, trying to pierce its

voice, as if attempting to find a gap to break through it. Sister Maria says the nightingale is 'all voice'. I know what she means: it's astonishing that such a small creature should have such a voluminous power of sound. It doesn't cheer me up. On the contrary, I feel sorry. At least if it had a smaller voice, I could bear it. The nightingale is bewildered by what comes out of its beak when it squeezes its little chest, a huge cloud of voice falls on top of it when it starts singing. What was the Lord God thinking of, imprisoning such a harmless little creature in its sonorous collapse, suffocating it beneath the weight of its voice?

I listen to the nightingale and hear only despair. But not because that poor creature lives an unhappy life. The nightingale is despairing over its very voice. It is horrified by the monstrosity that issues from its beak, it thinks it will free itself of its voice by hurling it out, it doesn't know that its vocal jet will never come to an end. It isn't like throwing up or coughing, which sooner or later comes to an end. The body cannot empty itself of its voice.

Today, with the violin, I tried to imitate the voice of the little birds. I was looking after the class of little ones, those of less than seven years. Now that I am sixteen, one of my tasks is to help teach the smallest. They learn on those tiny violins that produce very high-pitched sounds. With their tiny fingers they barely manage to guess one note in five, they're all out of tune. After a while they grow exasperated, it's obvious that they can't wait to grow up, to strengthen their grip. If they could they would lengthen their fingers with pincers to hasten their growth, they would pull them out from the palms of their hands.

Today I said to the little girls, 'Now let's imitate the sound swallows make.' I started scraping the strings of my violin with my bow.

The little girls frowned and blocked their ears.

'Come on, you try too!' I said.

Very shyly they began to stroke the strings, barely brushing them.

'Aren't you brave enough?'

It's surprising how these children are already trained to restrain themselves. As soon as you ask them to do anything out of the ordinary, they get timid.

'Come on, then! Haven't you ever heard a swallow? They don't whisper!'

We scattered around the room, running from one

corner to the other, with our bows scratching the ceiling, like the diagonal flight of swallows.

'Imagine you've just caught a mosquito in flight, with your beak wide open,' I said, running around the room, 'you've swallowed its blood-filled belly, you're telling the whole sky how good it is, you're yelling in the face of the blue that you're happy to be flying, you're drunk with dizziness, you're way up high, you're gliding, you're diving!' I was filling those graceful little bodies with excitement: 'Come on, little swallows, shriek, shriek!' The first sharp tones began to hum from their tiny violins, short at first, then deeper, more scraping screeches.

'What do you think you're doing?' The snake-haired head seldom talks to me so harshly.

'Have I made a mistake?'

'You've baffled those poor creatures. You've contaminated them with your anxieties.'

'I just wanted to get them out of their monotony. Make those children think the world is wider than they're used to thinking. That they can be different to what they are taught to imagine themselves to be.'

'There's great consolation in monotony. Habits cradle minds that have no other embrace to warm them. The world always presents itself in the same way, it isn't too painful, it doesn't add unexpected sufferings, it doesn't goad with inexplicable desires. You have trouble enough enduring yourself. Why overburden others with your pain?'

'But we were playing at imitating swallows! The little girls were enjoying themselves, they were laughing.'

'You presented them with your dissatisfactions, your yearning to be someone else.'

'I only wanted to give them joy!'

'They are vulnerable children. They can't bear the weight of unmotivated contentment.'

'You want them to live without openness, always doing the same things.'

'I want you not to compromise the grace of their spirit.'

'I taught them to fly! I let their souls take a breath of air.'

'You sowed only unease in them. From today they will be unhappier.'

'What am I supposed to do? What's the right thing? Hushing up the fact that there is a way that does not oppress us with the misery that surrounds us?'

The introduction to the last piece composed by Don Giulio was his usual dirge, a recapitulation of what he's been writing for fifty years, a kind of signature. The second part was all in unison. No counterpoint, no separation between melody and bass: all the instruments in chorus, the same notes, from the bassoon to the harpsichord to the violins. When we saw the score, my companions and I couldn't believe our eyes. Perhaps Don Giulio was trying to strengthen his music like that, crowding all the instruments into the same note, to fatten it up and make it more powerful. Instead, beneath the stave there were three ps, the sign for pianissimo. The adagio that followed was a hodgepodge of six or seven interwoven melodic lines, it was impossible to work out who was singing and who was accompanying, everyone had to play in a whisper, it was a tingle of weakness and sighs. The finale resumed with a ridiculous presto, consisting entirely of clauses, like someone saying goodbye a thousand times but without the courage to leave. At the end of the service I knew that the previous week he had been relieved of his position as composer and teacher at the Ospedale, and that this was his last concert here.

Lady Mother, I have kept the fist of my right hand

clenched for a good long time. The veins have fattened in my forearm. With the fingers of my left hand I pressed those string-like things that stood out under my skin, I played the part so many times that I will have to play during the service tomorrow. I have been practising all evening. My body is silent, but my mind, inside it, is full of sounds.

If we could play exactly what we are thinking, if our mind had a voice installed at the source of our thought sounds, we could destroy the earth from its root and build new mountains and new stars.

Lady Mother, today Sister Teresa came into the rehearsal room asking some of us to follow her. There were five of us, Maddalena, Gabriella, Elisabetta, Anita and me. They made us take our instruments. They made us wear the red dresses that we put on for public concerts. We wrapped ourselves up in our cloaks, under our hoods our faces were covered by masks. They opened for us the door at the back of the Ospedale, which gives onto the water, we got into a boat that was waiting for us. We felt the boatman's eyes on our backs, and the eyes of passers-by scanning us from the banks.

We entered a building, they made us climb the stairs. We passed through a drawing-room, we found ourselves in a room, the light was faint, the air was stale. We took off our cloaks, we kept on our masks. We sat down on two chairs and a stool. Elisabetta and Anita, the two singers, stayed standing. In the other corner of the room, lying on his bed, there was a man, if the word could still be applied to that core of dry skin scattered with dark stains. Close to the bed, bending over him, a priest and, I think, a doctor, or a relative, whispered in his ear. A third person was seated at a desk, dressed in elegantly austere clothes, he had a pen and some sheets of paper in front of him. They were all very old.

'They're here,' I thought I heard someone whisper.

My eyes wandered from one face to the other in the room, behind my impassive mask, in the gaps that opened like a pair of locks.

We took the instruments from their cases, at a nod from Sister Teresa we started playing, performing the pieces agreed with her on the boat-journey.

I saw the priest whispering in the ear of the old man lying on the bed, then he had a whispered conversation with the doctor and the person sitting at the desk, also involving Sister Teresa, who shook her head. Unable to

hear what they were saying, during this conversation I
was able to follow the conflicts between the faces and
the expressions they wore. The priest suggested, the
nun refused, the doctor, or relative if that's what he was,
pleaded, the nun grew indignant. In the end Sister Teresa
approached us with an unheard-of request.

'Take off your masks,' she said to us.

I looked at the four pairs of eyes in the slits in the masks
around me, my companions didn't know what to do.
Then, when Sister Teresa nodded again to assure us that
we hadn't misunderstood, and Maddalena put her hands
to the back of her neck, the rest of us also undid the knots
in the straps behind our heads. It was the first time I had
appeared naked in front of a man, if one excepted Don
Giulio and those few old priests who had seen my face.

Eyebrows were raised on those rough faces. They looked
at us. My face was sculpted by their eyes. My precious
intimacy, which is worth nothing. My secret, preserved
at the surface. Who are you? What power do you have
over us?

'This man is dying,' Sister Teresa said to us, as if defending herself for a crime. 'For years he has come and heard the services in our church, he is a devoted benefactor. He wanted to look you in the face just once. There's no harm in it.' Then she started moving the chairs and the stool, approaching the bed.

We played with our faces uncovered, our cheeks blazing. I was very sweaty inside my clothes, tied right up to the neck, I wished I could sink into the ground, I felt so powerless, at the mercy of those old men's eyes.

The priest seemed satisfied with the way things were going, the austere gentleman sitting at the desk picked up paper and pen and went to stand by the dying man.

The air was heavy, it passed through our instruments and through the throats of Elisabetta and Anita as they sang, alternating solos and duets. We tried to filter the air, scenting it with music, but it became increasingly malodorous.

I looked into the eyes of that desiccated head resting on its pillow, they were motionless. The lids were slightly unstuck from the eyes, like the collar of a shirt a size too big. I looked around for a spark of vitality in that gaze, a response to our performance. Playing like that, with our faces bared in front of someone, our music became something different to the usual: from pure autonomous fluid it became an effusion of our characters, an expression of us. Was that what that man wanted? To discover the source of the music? Or to know us a little better, the substance that had shaped us, the sound around which our bodies and our faces had grown, trained from birth in music?

I have been brought up with music, from the first day I was exposed to choruses and bows and strings and breaths and sounding boards, my body took shape around that musical fibre, that spinal column of sound.

Lady Mother, if I told you that that old man died as we were playing, my words would perhaps gain in solemnity, but I would probably be lying to you. I can't say with any certainty that he expired while we were playing for him. But were we playing for him, or was he dying for us? Who was more naked, who presented the more disarming spectacle? I played for I don't know how long, as though hypnotised, fixed on those two eyes that were perhaps looking at me, or were perhaps already dead; or perhaps they were looking at me all the more deeply precisely because they were already dead. We didn't accompany him into death, he was the one who made us resonate, who pulled the music out from a point within ourselves that we did not yet know. I couldn't say how long it took, but at some point the priest told us that it was enough. We tied our masks back on, we put the instruments back in their cases.

I would like to be able to play my violin inside its case, it too masked.

In the evening, leaning over the edge of the bed, Maddalena explained to me that the man sitting at the desk was a notary. A law of the republic requires notaries to remind anyone making a will of the orphans of our Ospedale, so that, if the dying man so wishes, he leaves part of his inheritance to the Ospedale. We had gone to play for money, in short. Money is even there before a dying man. It's always a question of money, of death and money. In church we play for alms and to finance the Ospedale, Jesus dies every day and we play at his funeral, for money.

Music, death and money. Money, death and music.

We are buried alive in a delicate coffin of music.

We stay behind these grilles, these latticed barriers, these bars of sonorous metal.

'It would seem that we have made the acquaintance of the real thing,' the snake-haired head said to me.

'Why are you talking to me like that?'

'At last you've seen a person dying. And how did it seem to you? Interesting?'

'Where did you get to?' I asked her, trying not to make her feel that I was happy to see her again.

'Why do you ask?'

'I've missed you.'

'Oh, I thought you did pretty well without me during that time.'

'What are you saying!'

'No, really! There are nights when you even manage to sleep. I don't want to disturb your dreams.'

'I never dream.'

'What do you know? Dreams vanish in the morning, you forget them.'

'I dream only of darkness. The black part of sleep, the one that fills your head when your eyelids close and you fall asleep.'

Lady Mother, I am in despair. Someone has discovered the letters I wrote to you and stolen them.

I wander the Ospedale like a damned soul. I pursue my tasks scrupulously, exaggerating my zeal. There is a lump in my throat from morning to evening. Today a cook blinded one of her eyes with a splash of boiling oil, and while I was being told I lowered my head as if it were my fault, I feel responsible for everything.

Time passes and no one calls me, no one tells me anything. I study my companions, I notice how they look at me, to work out if it was one of them. I try to read in their eyes whether they think I'm mad. Maybe they thought so even before they read my letters!

Three days have passed since my letters disappeared. I don't have the courage to ask. The nuns tell me nothing. The confessor tells me nothing. No one tells me anything. They leave me here to torture myself. Maybe it's their way of punishing me. They want to leave me in this state of suspension, of indecision, of suspicion. They want me to realise what I've done all by myself.

Lady Mother, in writing to you I was only speaking to a ghost. I was trying to restore a shape to a person who must not be in my life, who can't be there, who denied me, who clearly gave me to understand that I don't exist for her. By writing to you I touched with my hand the fact that I am nothing but a ghost.

At the Ospedale they welcomed me with open arms, but with these letters I reduced all their efforts to nothing. They have fed and clothed me, they have given me an education, they have taught me a trade, an art, they have given me everything and I repay them by complaining that I don't have near me the person who refused to give me anything at all since my first day of life. They have given me something bigger than a mother, they have given me the Lord God and music, they have taught me to make a particle of His glory vibrate with my frail hands, and I spend my time whinging.

They are turning me into a person when I would rather be a daughter.

Sister Teresa called me. She motioned me to follow her. 'Hurry up, we don't have much time,' she said. She led me to a part of the Ospedale where I had never been. In front of a door she looked around, to see if there was anyone in the corridor. We went inside. There were massive cupboards along the walls of the room. Sister Teresa asked me to turn round and close my eyes, which I did. I heard her going somewhere inside the room, then she said I could turn and look. I obeyed. Now she was holding a big, heavy key. She opened a cupboard. It was full of big books, files, bundles of papers tied with cloth ribbons, all diligently lined up. She took out a register. She set it down on one of the tables, she started quickly flicking through it, the frenzy of her movements stood out against all that order.

'Here, read this.'

Half-way down the page there was a date I knew very well. *Twenty-first of April. Wearing a green tunic*, it said. Sister Teresa opened an envelope that was stuck to the page, she took out a piece of paper: drawn on it was a lace fan, a ray of alternating coloured dots, green and blue. She pointed to a sentence on the page, beneath the fold of the envelope, which described that picture: *As a token, a piece of torn paper, half a wind-rose.* I felt tears welling up. Another note said: *the little girl was breathing badly, she was immediately baptised, with the name Cecilia.*

'That's all we know about you,' said Sister Teresa.

I burst out sobbing and hugged her. I smelled the smell of dust, her old-woman body.

'Come on, dear, let's get out of here. If they find us we're in terrible trouble,' she said, pulling gently away from me. 'They'll set us both to emptying the latrines, and you can forget about music!'

'What are you thinking about?' The head of black snakes whispered in my ear.

'What do you think I'm thinking about?'

'These are the times when you have to think about something else.'

'There isn't anything else.'

'You're too self-obsessed. The world is large.'

'Not for me.'

'You're such a whine.'

'It's the world I was thinking about.'

'You're wondering where she is, aren't you?'

'I'll never find her.'

'You've never lost her, you've never had her.'

Whole days walking in a state of suspense. I rest my footsteps on the shadow, I don't know where I am, what's consistent, whether I'm sinking or standing.

I breathe mechanically, I get out of bed mechanically, I eat mechanically, I play mechanically, I pray mechanically, perhaps I'm not doing any of these things, I don't know.

I've found my letters. In the hiding-place where I've always kept them. Someone let me find them. Sister Teresa, I imagine. Like a kind of absolution, of forgiveness. Am I supposed to think it's an encouragement to continue? Or an invitation to reread them? Or perhaps Sister Teresa and my spiritual directors are trying to make me understand that everything I do goes on under their eyes, that they follow my every step, so I must know that all my actions are being watched and judged. That's supposed to make me more responsible, I imagine. Don't do anything unbecoming. Bear in mind that everything you do is under the gaze of one who has the welfare of your soul at heart. Take care of yourself while remaining aware of the constant presence of that gaze. Which is not the gaze of the Lord God: how arrogant it would be to bother him just to watch us behaving stupidly.

The days pass without meaning. I get up, pray without knowing what I'm saying, let the words pass through me, drink a cup of something, rehearse old pieces of music with my companions, the sounds pass through my limbs without leaving a trace, it's as if the written notes were demanding to be heard, well then, I shall obey, if you really want me to, just do it, here it is, I'm playing without even listening to you. A new teacher of composition and violin has arrived. He's young, his nose is big and his hair is red. I teach the youngest girls, I show them how to hold the violin and move the bow. Yesterday one of them asked me if we were trying to imitate creaking doors with our instruments, another said she preferred miaowing cats. I hushed them, I delivered a lengthy reproach, I said that music is a serious thing, and doubled the number of exercises they have to study.

Lady Mother, you left my little body in the alcove of the Ospedale, wrapped in a green dress. The token that you left is half of a wind-rose. I don't think you will ever come back to the Ospedale and present yourself with the missing half, which fits perfectly with the one kept in the archive, to show that you are my mother and you have come to take your daughter back. You would have done it when I was a little girl, it's too late now.

Lady Mother, it's today that I really need you, throughout these years, now that I'm becoming a woman, something completely different from what I have been until now. The nuns can't help me in this. Even though Sister Teresa loves me, she knows nothing of what it means to be a woman. My companions have grown up in here, they have no idea what it means to be a woman either, they are poor frightened creatures. All that exists for them is music and wild fantasies, they imagine finding love, they dream of some son of a wealthy family asking for their hands in marriage. They want love, a family, to have children. They play from behind the grilles, thinking they are making their listeners fall in love with them. But the people who come to church to listen to us do it to dream, to have their own dreams.

The girls fantasise about some nice, rich boy coming to take them away. The young men who listen to us in church imagine faces that don't exist, they're infatuated by them. In this world everyone is in love with his fantasy.

We swap our fantasies. We expect flesh-and-blood people to fall within the profile of the adored image that we have fantasised to our own measure, we want them to wear it like a second skin which transfigures their features and their stature.

Lady Mother, what if the colour of the dress I was wearing when you left me here was no accident? And if the colours of the wind-rose that you left as a token had a meaning too? I think of nothing else, from morning till evening, I've been mulling it over at night, too, for days, for weeks. I've been trying to interpret the hidden message that you might have been trying to hide in those colours. Green, blue. You delivered me wrapped in a green blouse. There was the same colour on the token of recognition, in the greenish-blue rays of the wind-rose that I saw in the register, on the page of my birth. Each ray consisted of two paired pointers, one green and one blue. But if the token is torn in two, it means that the part preserved in the archive represents me, I'm the part that has stayed in the Ospedale. So the missing part is you. I was dressed in green, I'm the green part. You're the blue part. The wind-rose was cut diagonally, like this: Ø. The remaining half points north-west. The missing half is you, the other colour, you are blue, you are the other side of each ray of the wind-rose, paired with me, the colour green. You are the cropped part, the one facing south-east. Yes, it must be that, I'm sure it's that. You left by sea, towards the blue, to the south-east! Towards Dalmatia, or Greece. I stayed in the north-west, on earth, where the grass grows, you brought me here dressed in green. You abandoned me because you had to leave, to flee towards one of our republic's possessions, on the Slavic Sea, or the Greek one. Or else you left precisely because you abandoned me, you went away after my birth. But you wanted to leave me with a clue of the direction you took.

At the moment I'm not thinking about anything else, I'm hypothesising like mad, imagining countless scenarios, and always at the centre of all my fantasies is you, that empty outline bringing me into the world, detaching itself from me, fleeing into the distance.

I came into the world from the void.

A hollow niche, a missing portion of space, a subtraction, a small amount of nothing is my mother.

This was the fate I was given, to be the daughter of nothing.

I think I've glimpsed the truth and am elated, then I bring myself back down telling myself it's all mere illusions, fantasies, I'm placing too much importance on a piece of rag paper, on the colours of a torn drawing and a piece of clothing that no longer exists. But what should I do? I'm left with the image of half a sheet of paper that I glanced at for a few moments, and the description of a piece of clothing, it's all I have, it's all I know about me, it's all I know about you.

We play the music of men. Almost all the musicians are priests.

Men invade us with their music. Don Antonio, the new violin teacher and composer at the Ospedale, brings us the music that he has written, we read his score, we copy out our parts, and that way the music starts to insinuate itself within us, we follow it with our eyes. The music makes our writing arm move, we study it. Then we hold our instruments. Don Antonio's music comes in through our eyes, impregnates our heads, makes our arms move. The elbows and wrists of our right arms loosen to work the bow, the fingers of our left hands bend on the strings. We are run through by the music of men.

Lady Mother, by now I know this building as I know my own mind. I remember to perfection the length of the corridors, the number of stairs, the distance between one door and the other. Mine is not a simple intellectual memory, but physical, engraved within my body, my legs, as they part to take a step of precisely the right length, repeated exactly the number of times necessary to cover the diagonal of a room, it is a memory stamped in my hand, which reaches out blindly, gripping the handle precisely, without knocking its knuckles against the door or being left in mid-air with a fistful of flies. Over the years I have learned to cross the Ospedale with my eyes closed, thinking it, imagining it. And my imagination corresponds to the reality. The length of my steps is the right one, the lifting of my foot to climb the step is neither too high nor too low. I think about how to move, in which direction, and how much to move, and the Ospedale corresponds to the movement steered by my thought. The Ospedale is a thought of mine.

''You're losing contact with reality.'

'What should I do?'

'You think everything is the fruit of your thought. Your mother, your life, your birth. Now the Ospedale, too.'

'You are the fruit of my thought as well.'

'Indeed. I won't show myself again.'

'Don't you leave me too!'

The snake-haired head doesn't reply.

'Don't leave me…!'

Lady Mother, don't take offence, but there are nights when I go and talk to my other mother. I've never told you, even though I assume you already suspect as much. I get up from my bed and walk through the Ospedale plunged in sleep. It's the dead of night, the darkest hour, the one when the darkness crowds most densely in on itself. I move eyes closed along the corridors, I reach the stairs, I climb the steps, I run my hand along the metal of the banister, I recognise all its tiny imperfections, I reach the last little door, I open it and feel the space throwing itself open. I am inside the church. I find myself on the balcony a few metres up, where we are used to playing behind the grilles that hide our features.

The dark church is inhabited by the Mother of God. I can't see her in the nocturnal gloom, but I know she's there, on the altar, painted on the altarpiece. I'm invisible too, plunged in darkness, a darkness so dense that I'm amazed the air has preserved its lightness.

Lady Mother, once I brought my violin with me to play in the darkness of the deserted church. I'm always immersed in music, music never stops resounding in my mind, so I wanted to offer it to you, my other mother. I passed through the Ospedale, I opened the little door, I sat down on the balcony that protrudes from the wall, suspended in the air. Everything was in darkness. I felt the space stretching out in front of me, above and below me, filled with black air. The same air that I breathe licked the cheek of the Mother of God painted on the altarpiece. I was so excited! Everything within me was tumultuous, outside it was perfectly calm. I offered my tumult to the Mother of God and went on experiencing it. I thought it better to let the Mother of God listen to what was going on within my soul, the music that I was composing inside me, without needing to play it.

I was prudent, without wishing to be so. If I had played my violin in church at night, sooner or later someone would have found me out. But no one can hear the secret music that plays in our souls. No one can keep it from sounding within us. No one can steal it.

Men organise ceremonies, they get themselves up in gleaming robes, they tinkle precious metals, they set the glory of the words in sweetly rhythmical phrases, they fill the air with scented smoke and music, they need to put everything outside, they have to expel, always expel from themselves, whatever it is that they feel inside.

We girls aren't allowed to express what pullulates within our souls. And yet we too are filled with sounds. The Mother of God hears what is happening within us. She doesn't need us to play our music.

Today I no longer think like that, today I'm just obeying the law of the Ospedale. The world wants us to be silent. And if we think that music still echoes in our souls, and consider it more true than what we hear with our ears, in the air, outside our bodies, then all we are doing is listening to those who want us to be quiet.

Why are there no women musicians? Why do women not compose music? Why do they merely allow it to resonate within their souls, tormenting them, corroding their thoughts? Why do they not free themselves of it by expelling it? What would happen if the world were invaded by the sounds that occur within the souls of women?

So that night in the church I set aside my violin and sat in silence. Or rather, from outside it seemed as if I were in silence, while a hundred instruments played within me. I started playing music with my mind. Inside me, my violin dived into the stormy waves of sound, vanished from the surface and re-emerged like a dolphin used to dwelling in tempests.

I sat down on the balcony inside the church, facing infinite black space, beneath the depths of the sky, hanging over the abyss, in the silence of my breath. The black air enters me and leaves without a sound, I hear the sweet inner

backwash of my blood, the calm spasm of my heartbeat.
I play my body.

I go to find the Mother of God at the end of the night,
when the darkness is deepest. I cross the Ospedale, I walk
down the corridors, I delicately open and close the doors,
I climb the stairs, I appear in the empty church, I sit down
on the balcony, behind the balustrade, behind the grille,
in the darkness, hanging in the void. When dawn begins
to filter in, illuminating the face of the Mother of God, I
get to my feet and return to my bed.

'I'm jealous.'
   'That's why I haven't heard from you!'
   'I admit it. I'm honest, I'm not hiding my envy of your
second mother.'
   'Who?'
   'The one you allow to listen to the music that you hear
sounding within you.'
   'Would you like me to play for you too?'
   'I don't know.'
   'Are you too ashamed to ask me for requests?'
   The head of black snakes gives a hint of a laugh. 'I
know how great my strength is, I am running no risk in

showing you a bit of weakness.'

'If you tell me where we can meet, I can try and play for you too.'

'I don't know.'

'You come and find me in the greatest variety of places, without warning, but if you give me an appointment, I'll let you hear my music.'

'I don't know.'

'You don't want to?'

'I'm frightened.'

'You? I don't believe you!'

'I fear for you. The music you would think in my presence would make you scream with terror, you'd go mad.'

I left my room, I crossed the Ospedale and I opened the little door leading onto the balcony. I walked to the grille. The church was plunged in darkness. I concentrated to let my musical prayer spring forth within me. For the moment, I felt the beats of my heart. First one, then the other, then yet another. It was as if they wanted to come out, echoing in the empty space. What was happening? My heart was resounding inside the church! I grew frightened. The church was a musical box, designed to exalt any embellishment of the air, rendering audible even the cry of an ant. But I certainly couldn't have imagined that it was capable of amplifying the beats of the heart. Perhaps the black air had a secret intimacy with the hidden depths of a heart buried within the breast. Then I worked out that it wasn't in fact the beats of my heart, but footsteps. I wasn't alone. Someone was walking inside the church.

The person walking in the darkness must have entered the church via the sacristy. It seemed to me that they were heading towards the back wall, towards the altar. It must have been someone who knew the space well, just as I knew the Ospedale. Another person who, like me, was able to move in the darkness, measuring distances without stumbling.

With the help of my imagination I located the sound of those footsteps, inside that plain little church. Four walls, with an altar on the back wall, up a short flight of steps.

Then the footsteps returned from whence they had come, going back inside the sacristy. I heard a drawer moving. A key turned in a little lock, a panel was opened. I pricked up my ears till they hurt. Perhaps I dreamt it, in those hallucinated hours, in the deep darkness, but I thought I heard the rustle of a hand running over a fabric incrusted with embroidery. I imagined hard, symmetrical, gilded veins, in relief on a rather stiff fabric. The rustle grew in volume through the air, an enveloping swish. Someone was enrobing himself.

The footsteps came back towards the altar. It was then that my doubts came to an end. A man was murmuring in the dark. He was celebrating mass in the gloom.

I stayed to listen to those beautiful words. He was whispering as if distracting himself from their significance because the sounds writhed in his mouth of their own accord. The liturgy unfolded like a dream. All of a sudden I noticed that the celebrant was uttering a brief homily. Were we already at that point in the mass? Or was it the priest who had interrupted the service?

'Lord, I am a bad priest,' said the celebrant. 'I have but a small voice, I do not have the strength to make myself heard. I don't know how to preach. All I want to offer by way of words is the music that they make in the mouth, even when our voice speaks, calmly, without singing.'

Dawn was beginning to filter through the windows. The shadows withdrew. The light delineated the first shapes, waking them. It chose which features of the world would have priority, which outlines were to emerge before the others. It stroked objects, as if wishing to accustom them to the violence that the morning would soon be committing upon them, exposing them to total nakedness.

I saw the celebrant from behind, facing the altar. He had reached the moment of consecration. His gestures were strange. I felt as if he were surprised to witness the things that he himself was doing. He had found himself with a piece of bread in his hand and his arms raised aloft.

For a few moments he couldn't work out what he had done, how on earth he had ended up in that position.

Then, of their own accord, his hands gripped a gold cup and raised it up as well. The priest lowered it, sniffing the contents of the cup. An acid vapour must have befuddled him.

He had just consecrated the bread and wine. He had transformed them into the flesh and blood of the Lord

God. Or rather, the Lord God had sneaked His way into a miserable piece of bread, a cup of poor-quality wine. The priest shivered. He must have had a sense of how sinful it was, all this. A god that becomes some milled seeds and fermented fruit juice. How he is chewed and digested inside the foul bellies of human beings.

He didn't want to think of the Lord God's journey inside his intestines, and what would come out at the end of its sordid passage through his body.

I identified with his anxiety. I heard him say these words, or perhaps I imagined them: 'Why did the Lord God want to become this? Wasn't it enough for him to be made flesh only once? Why did he want to be reincarnated thousands of times inside our bodies, to undergo this humiliation, infinitely more inglorious than death on the cross, a thousand times worse than being whipped and spat upon, and mocked and murdered like a criminal? Why this *via crucis* within our bowels?'

Through the window the first light of day poured into the church.

The priest looked at what he was holding in his fingers. A crust of bread. Half a cup of wine. He put the bread in his mouth. He knew he wasn't supposed to chew it: the body of the Lord God was not to be insulted in that way.

He pushed it in, towards his throat. The mouthful wouldn't go down. He swallowed, lowering his chin to his neck to reinforce the grip of his muscles. He closed his throat. He coughed. He struck himself on the chest, with his hand. He went on coughing. The mouthful was stuck in his throat. He couldn't breathe. He bent over the altar, gasping for breath. He collapsed.

'Don Antonio, Don Antonio!' I heard an old woman's voice from the sacristy, then I saw Sister Apollonia running towards the altar.

'Asthma, asthma!' the nun said. 'What a stubborn man he is, he knows he's not supposed to say mass!'

'It went down the wrong way…' the priest managed to whisper between convulsions. 'I'm short of breath…'

The nun started slapping him hard on the back, vigorous claps, as Don Antonio went on coughing.

The church echoed with that strange, ungainly rhythm.

It was the prayer of the priest's body: coughing fits and blows on his body, which refused to digest the Lord God and turn Him into dung.

Sister Apollonia played on that breathless drum, a goatskin emitting puffs of air, little voiceless explosions.

The priest felt something harsh being poured into his mouth.

He opened his eyes, he saw that the old nun was making him drink the contents of the gilded metal cup.

'But it's the...!' the priest protested, thinking that swallowing the blood of the Lord God to unblock a mouthful of God Himself that had gone down the wrong way might be considered a sacrilege.

'Drink, drink,' the nun said. 'The good God will be pleased to have saved you with His blood. Swallow it down without fear!'

I witnessed that scene as if I were experiencing a dream that had gradually emerged from the dark depths of night. I felt as if I myself were that priest.

I spend my life in a state of total detachment, I don't care a jot about others, I can't take an interest in the concerns of my companions, I don't take part in their disputes, I don't listen to their gossip. Then all of a sudden I plunge into someone. I feel what he feels, I experience his sensations, I empathise. You, Lady Mother, Sister Teresa, the newborn kittens, the Mother of God, and now Don Antonio, too.

Lady Mother, something strange has been happening to me for a few weeks now. Have you noticed? As I was writing to you, almost without noticing the letters turned themselves into notes. A phrase becomes a melody, a word is accompanied by its counterpoint. I surprise myself composing on paper, spontaneously, transcribing a thought that was born as a discourse and transforms itself into a sound.

Rereading the letters that I have written to you, including the ones returned to me, I marked sequences of notes above some of the passages, turning the things that I have to say to you into recitatives to be sung to a harpsichord accompaniment, elaborating them into airs and motets.

The thought and the word that names it make a musical

accord, they are like two notes played at the same time, sometimes harmoniously, sometimes out of tune.

The sound of a word and its meaning make a musical accord, the phrase unravels as a counterpoint.

The meaning is the *basso continuo* of a word. Sometimes the tune of a word fits harmoniously with its meaning, sometimes it's inappropriate, it shrieks. Sometimes a phrase clashes ingeniously with the concept it expresses.

We played one at a time in the room, to be judged by the new teacher of composition. Don Antonio listened sitting down, with his back to us, so as not to be influenced by our appearance. What power lies within the faces and bodies of women, which means that they cannot show themselves even when they are doing something else, not even when they are playing, or else their appearance conquers all and confuses the judgement even of the most dispassionate souls?

My companions were very excited. In reality, making a good immediate impression on the new composer was of little consequence. It will be daily practice that will reveal our true worth. But they don't want to miss an opportunity to stand out. They have nothing else in life.

When my turn came, Sister Agata called me into the room, I entered and stood in front of the nun who was writing our names in the register. Beside her was Don Antonio who, as I have said, had his back to me. Without taking her eyes off me, the old nun brought her lips close to the long copper-coloured hair of the young priest, and whispered a few words in his ear. I waited in silence for a few moments, then improvised a piece that was little more than childish, one of the ones you give little girls to study less than a year after they first pick up the violin. I played looking at that nape and those two curtains of reddish hair that seemed to catch my notes like a metal spider's web. Towards the end of my piece I played a note out of tune, I did it on purpose, because I don't want to be praised, I don't want to be singled out, I want to stay in the background. So, in the middle of some phrasing that was already quite dreadful, I made a howler, but not so emphatic as to be taken as a caricature.

I was following the youngest ones, in the afternoon,

when Don Antonio came into the room. 'So, girls, is your teacher good?'

'I'm not a teacher,' I observed. 'I'm still too young. I just lend a hand with their exercises for a few hours in the afternoon.'

'Let them reply,' Don Antonio said to me with a smile.

'She is good, but not like that time when she made us be little birds!' said Elena, the youngest one.

'Little birds?' said the priest, and he pulled a slightly excessive grimace, exaggerating his surprise.

'Yes! She made us make the voices of swallows with our violins, and she played like the nightingale does!'

'And you liked it?'

'Yes, lots! But she won't let us do it again.'

'It was just to show them how not to use a violin and...' I mumbled.

'Let me hear a little bit,' Don Antonio broke in.

The little girls couldn't believe it, they started doing swallows by drawing shrill screeches from the strings, as they had done a month ago, but much more wildly, as if they hadn't forgotten and couldn't wait to do it again.

'And the nightingale?'

'Only she knows how to do that one!' said the little girls.

Don Antonio looked at me. 'Come on, what are you waiting for,' he said to me.

I made a few embellishments, lazily, putting in my usual wrong notes.

'Don't try and pull that one on me again,' said the priest. 'That's a wrong note that's trying to imitate a wrong note. Just like the other day, when I tested you. It's the mediocre way of playing that only someone who plays to perfection can fake.'

I do everything I can think of to take an interest in the other girls who live with me at the Ospedale, but I can't do it. I set myself the task of understanding their thoughts, their wishes, but as soon as I listen to them for more than five minutes I get distracted, I think of something else. And yet, who knows, one of them might be like you, within them I could find a way of thinking that could help me understand you. By putting together lots of little details taken from my companions, perhaps I could reconstruct you, Lady Mother.

The score that Don Antonio gave us for rehearsals this morning left us speechless.

'It's unfinished!'

'There's a movement missing!'

'There are only three parts, rather than four!'

'There's no introductory adagio!'

'It starts with a presto!'

My companions were scandalised, they were muttering about it today at the Ospedale, no one was talking about anything else, but the nuns didn't bat an eyelid: 'If this is what the maestro has written, this is what you must play.'

He wooed them well, that young man. Now here he is with twenty mummies who always leap to his defence.

I haven't been as clever as that in all those years. I couldn't get anyone to adopt me. I couldn't invent a reserve mother for myself. I have been faithful to you, Lady Mother, faithful in my resentment and bitterness, faithful in my spite and my grievances, faithful in my recrimination and my insults.

'You're unfair. There is someone who's adopted you.'

'You want me to thank you for your frightening apparitions?' I say to the snake-haired head.

'Don't be cross with me. But there are lots of people here who love you.'

'Who?'

'You should know,'

'Sister Teresa?'

'Don't ask me, ask the things themselves.'

'Does the Mother painted on the altar love me?'

'Do you still go to her to let her listen to the music that flows in your mind?'

'Every night.'

'Then you love her. That's what matters.'

'What?'

'Affection. Giving love, not receiving it. Loving, not being loved.'

'I thought you were much more disenchanted. Harder.'

'Ah, but it's much more disenchanted to love than to be loved. Expecting nothing from anyone.'

I don't know which saint we're celebrating today, we're supposed to be playing Don Antonio's concertos for the first time in public.

The church is full of heads, from up above I can see nothing but heads peering towards our balustrades, the pomp of their hairdos. I hear the rustle of the luxurious fabrics, the murmur of expectation. Don Antonio smiles, he nods, we start. I glanced down, peering beyond the grille to see what effect he had created by setting off at a rush like that, without the introduction of the initial adagio, I had a sense of necks stiffening and ears pricking, caught by surprise.

Those dozens of ears sitting in the depths of the church accompanied us with their silence, they were part of the orchestra. The heads sunk in musical attention are the principal instruments in the performance. You only really play in public, there is no music without a crowd of ears to support it.

Lady Mother, how can I make you hear what we played? Do you know how to read music? All I can do is make use of images. I thought I was sprinkling powder on the heads of the men sitting on the church benches. We scattered our perfumed powder, our feminine spice over those people. Don Antonio has written a concerto in which you can hear our womanly character frothing, in three phases, first gaiety, then languor, then euphoria again. This man draws feminine sounds from our bodies, he gives old men's age-plugged ears the sound version of women, our translation into sounds, as men want to hear it. And yet, as I say this I'm not being entirely honest. Today, even more than I guessed during rehearsals, I felt I was doing something more, Don Antonio was pushing us, he was making us overflow beyond ourselves, we were plunging from the balustrades, there was something beyond the usual graceful pose, beyond the frivolity required from our concerts, a more frenzied, shameless intensity, in the fast movements, and an unseemly, disconsolate unease in the central adagio.

This music is made of woman, we scatter our spiced perfume in the air, is that what Don Antonio wants?

Today, at rehearsals, Don Antonio asked us if we had ever seen the beautiful season in the countryside.

Giovanna, the cellist, said that when she was little, before her parents died, she remembered...

'Well, I'm sorry but this time we'll have to do without you,' Don Antonio broke in.

He sent her from the room, going with her in person. He went in search of another girl to take her place, then started interrogating us again.

'None of you have ever seen spring in the countryside?'

'No.'

'Not even once?'

'We grew up in here. We have been on boat-trips between the islands, but we have never travelled through the countryside.'

'Would you like to see the world in bloom?'

'Yes!'

'Well, get ready.'

He disappointed us. He made us think he was organising an outing for us, to places we had never seen, where we had never been, and all this not as a reward, but for the purposes of study, as a preparation for work, to make us hear the sounds of the earth and the sky and make us play better, and instead he tricked us.

'Very good, my precious ones. Now we will travel through the world and time. In our imagination. You will become everything. Kindness and fury. You have everything within you. Do you also have the courage for it? Are you ready?'

He has written a pastiche of sounds imitating the noises of the seasons. He has copied the idea that I had in class with the little girls.

The two little musical phrases at the beginning of the spring concerto close with a longer note, a shrieking swallow. Its cry cuts the air, it slices the sky to pour floods of new air through the wound.

'Don't be so graceful, make the swallow screech at the end of the phrase!' Don Antonio told us at rehearsals.

In the first notes you hear the swallows arriving. Then warmth swells in the air, the water is freed from the ice and flows away, suddenly a storm silences the birds, but it doesn't last long, the shepherd snores after dinner, the dog barks, there's dancing before sunset, men and women having a party...

'Don Antonio, what's a ball?'

'I've never seen one.'

'How do men and women dance together?'

'I don't know.'

'And how can we play it if we don't even know it?'

'How would you like it to be? How do you imagine men and women being happy together?'

'Here you're supposed to hear peasants playing bagpipes,' says Don Antonio, pointing to a page in the score.

'What are they?'

'Bags full of breath, gripped under the arm, as the air

comes out it whistles one note that's always the same, while on another reed the fingers block and open the holes.'

'But we have only stringed instruments!'

'I want you to make me hear the bag with a hole in it losing its breath.'

'With violins and violas?'

It's a constant play of disguise, of pretending not to be what we are, of imitating instruments that we have never heard and don't possess. We pretend not to play what we're playing, to go beyond our means through those very means. We make our violins sound like things and landscapes, animals and noises, and even other instruments, and even other violins, tormented, played badly by peasants scraping on them as they hop from one leg to another, after drinking too much.

...the cuckoo and the turtledoves insist, the sparrows quarrel, the wind stretches out, heavier and heavier, a young peasant starts crying, weariness falls after work, the flies, the hornets, thunder rumbles away in the distance, swoops down on the countryside, we become the storm! We are the storm, the storm explodes, we lay waste, we smash the fine weather!

'Smash the fine weather! Smash the fine weather! Louder! You're the storm! Become a tempest, girls, become a tempest!'

And I have been all of this, storm, tempest, thunder, lightning, I have wept as I felt myself becoming so much rage, going beyond myself. I was moved to find myself turned into so many things, and I felt sorry for myself, without self-pity. I have wept not to be able to be simply myself, when I can be so many other things, so loud, I who would ask nothing but to be able to say I am here, I am Cecilia, I am all here.

He has written four poems, one for each season, he has had them printed and distributed in church, before the concert, to teach his audience how to listen, to make them imagine with the music, like dreaming with their eyes open. He's a cheat, an impostor. He contaminates the purity of the music with children's toys.

At the start of each of the four concertos, before the music, he insisted on the explanatory lines being read out loud.

'Spring has come, and the birds greet it with sounds of celebration...'

He taught Barbara to read the legends written on the score, during the concerto of the seasons, in church, proclaiming it in a loud voice.

'The air opens up. The birds learn to sing again. The ice melts, the water has lost its shape.'

'The herdsman huddles against his goats. The dog barks at something in the distance. The shepherds dance as they can.'

'The heat makes it impossible to breathe. Here is the cuckoo, turtledove calls to turtledove, a goldfinch joins in.'

'A storm threatens from far off. The mountain wind comes, it will devastate everything. The young peasant weeps with rage.'

'Flies, everywhere. The storm explodes.'

'The peasants dance and sing. This one has drunk too

much. He sways, he sleeps on his feet.'

'The beast escapes. Rifles, dogs. The beast is injured, it dies.'

'The wind is frightening. Warming yourself by stamping your feet on the ground, shivering, teeth chattering.'

'Rain, all is rain.'

'Walking on the ice, being careful. Slipping, falling, crashing. The ground creaks beneath your feet.'

'All the icy winds, all at once.'

I imagine how the listeners must have taken it. Hail fell heavily from our furious musical balustrades. Music was thrown on their heads by the bucketful, they listened to all that a human being can live through in a year, the experiences that he can have while contemplating the world and being submerged in it, the hot and the cold, the exhaustion and the intoxication. But we who played it didn't simply listen to them, those things ran through us.

Lady Mother, if I told you that I was all those things, that I was the birds and the storm and all the rest, I would not be honest. It would be naivety or imposture. I was that musical tradition of those things, I was the whole world in a violinist version. And yet, even so, that blast of universe ran through me, it moved the whole of me. What I would like to make you understand is that I too was inside it, I heard the orchestra playing around me, and I was part of it.

I have been pierced by time and space, and by all the things that they carry within them. In the end I was exhausted, in the course of an hour I had been musically hail, musically sultriness, musically chill, musically warmth, musically stamped feet, musically light rain, musically frozen ground that hurts when you fall on it, musically soft meadow, I had been musically inside the sleep of a goatherd, inside a barking dog, inside the eyes of a fly, musically I have been black fog, drunken footstep, terrified beast and the bullet that kills it.

The only thing that could musically enter the lightning was Don Antonio's violin, with his frantic bow. The sky's bow-string yearns, possessed by an idea. To go to vibrate, to be the tremulousness in the heart of the secret, there's a crack in the world, the spring of creation rips and floods with light.

In an hour, living musically, playing with your own body and your own spirit, pierced by a gale, immersed in the playing orchestra, being part of it, listening and at the same time contributing to the making of the clamour and the silences. In an hour, living everything that can happen to a human being.

We are condemned to abstraction. Through our bodies passes this idea that doesn't exist outside of us, which we call music.

It is so childish to start imitating the sounds of the world by playing music, when the only thing capable of imitating music is our ideas.

Music is the thing closest to a pure idea.

Music is the idea made thing outside of us.

In the end, nothing but tomfoolery. The seasons! Spring,

summer, autumn and winter aped by musical instruments. Music in masks. How shameful.

Lady Mother, I am defending myself against what I have seen while playing this music, only a few hours have passed and already I am starting to speak ill of it, to protect myself from the emotions that it has made me feel.

The whole city has been conquered by the concertos on the seasons.

'Girls, the governors of the Ospedale have asked me for something else equally powerful. We will play this city's greatest fear. A storm at sea, ships that are about to be wrecked but then…'

'It's so childish to imitate the sounds of the world,' a voice interrupted. 'The only things that music can imitate are our ideas.' It was I who spoke thus.

My impertinence created silence in the rehearsal room. My companions seemed to be paralysed. Even Sister Marianna couldn't react, such was her consternation. The only one who wasn't dismayed was Don Antonio.

'You're right, it's the stupidest thing I've written, but

it's what I need to reach everyone's ears,' he replied. 'We have to be humble enough to make ourselves understood. We have to use our complication to draw simplicity cleverly out.'

After the success of the concertos on the seasons, Don Antonio thinks he's in a position to do everything. He comes to the Ospedale like a braggart. He demands that the cellists take their instruments out of their laps.

'It isn't a baby!' he says. 'You're supposed to be playing music, not playing with dolls.'

'Then how do we hold them?'

'Vertically, resting on the ground.'

'And what about our legs? It's impossible.'

'Make some room and grip it hard between your knees, so that you don't let it fall.'

'With our legs open? But that's not seemly!'

'No one can see you. You're behind the balustrade, when you play in public, up at the top.'

This time the nuns were perplexed, they reported this new development to the governors of the Ospedale.

'No one will see them,' Don Antonio repeated.

'If word gets out about this eccentricity, there will be protests, some people will be scandalised.'

'Why?'

'They will say that we are not bringing up our girls to be modest. The other Ospedali in the city will compete with us, they will convince their benefactors that it is better to donate their money to those who bring up more serious girls...'

'...and inferior musicians,' replied Don Antonio.

'You must act with discernment.'

'Where's the harm in it? They have to play with as much ease as possible. The instrument isn't a dead child.'

'But it isn't... it isn't a husband, either, if you'll forgive me, Don Antonio! If this reaches the ears of...'

'What will reach the ears is how our cellists will be able to play, with their hands much freer to run up and down the strings. You will hear how fast are their fingers.'

In the instrument there are not dead children, but trees felled and cut in pieces, there are animals gutted to pull out their bowels, dry them, twist and stretch them. Sound-boxes and strings. Within my violin lies the voice of forests killed and animals butchered. We are playing the funeral of nature, we are holding its corpse.

Don Antonio wants to have holes dug in the corners of the walls of the church at the height of the balustrades, openings where the choir is to be arranged so that the voice arrives from all directions, shot from the fiery mouths of the singers, to merge in the middle of the church, interweaving, like gusts of opposing winds, marine currents, arguments, longings.

Yesterday we played for the King of Denmark. The sovereign wanted to remain incognito, but the clumsy respects of an ambassador involuntarily made his visit public. So the aristocracy and the state found themselves obliged to pay their respects to him, and he had to put up with official feasts, when he would much rather have discovered the forbidden side of the city. We are part of the official side, we are a piece of institution, we swell the ranks of boredom. That is the role entrusted to us. We see them, through the grilles, the noblemen who snort as they listen to us, the ladies yawning.

There are those who impersonate rectitude in such a way as to make its opposite stand out with still greater clarity. That's the purpose we serve. Sometimes I wonder whether the people who come to hear us, to whom we are pointed out as models of virtue, do it with the sole intention of finding vice yet more enjoyable when they leave this place. We raise their spirits, they climb up so that they can throw themselves into the abyss of perdition from an even higher place, making their dive all the more intoxicating.

Today Don Antonio brought us another new concerto. We crowded around the score, we flicked avidly through it, full of curiosity, anticipating the new adventure that we were about to experience. In a few minutes, disappointment appeared on our faces.

'But... it's the same as last week's...'

'It *seems* the same, girls.'

'The melodic line is practically the same. And the rhythm, too...'

'But the instruments are different. The distribution of the parts is different.'

'How so?'

'I wanted to see what would happen if instead of entrusting this tune to the violin I gave it to an oboe—' Before continuing with his speech, Don Antonio looked me in the eyes. 'Is it still the same idea if we play it like this? We don't need to let things happen only within us.

We have to help them come into the world as best we can, rethink them, rewrite them, play them differently.'

Yesterday they loaded us into the boat for another trip. They treat us like horses, made to trot in the open air so that they don't go mad. We ended up on an island that I had never seen before. Two old peasants, a man and a woman, offered us their new wine. The nuns were against it, but then they were the first to try a sip. It's a brackish liquid, grown on the sands, it absorbs saliva, it leaves the tongue dry. We played and sang for that old couple. Sitting side by side, they listened to us. In the end those two old people treated us almost as if we were magicians. They who have lived through every hardship revered us who know nothing of life, save how to move our fingers over some animal gut tied over a wooden box. It isn't right. They asked permission to touch our instruments, they didn't know that there were things in the world that produced such strange sounds. They were also impressed by the throats of the singers. The old woman touched the neck of Serena, the contralto, with the same reverent astonishment that she lavished on my violin. 'Uh, uh...' she too attempted, with a hoarse wheeze. She was behaving like an old animal, I think she felt like a monkey confronted by a superior being. She had never heard such singing, by voices as properly trained as ours. I don't know whether to be happy to have brought music to that island, into the ears of those two old people who had perhaps never listened to it in their lives. I wonder which is better, whether or not to know that there's another way of being in the world, when they can no longer experience it. We ruined their peace. Those two old people had managed to pass through life unharmed by the promise that music makes, they will die sadder than they were before they listened to us.

Lady Mother, it's lesson day today. The daughters of the rich come here and learn to scrape. We sit down in little rooms: violin, harpsichord, flute. I'm still too young to give private lessons, but they keep me here so that I can learn to teach.

The daughters of the rich who come into the Ospedale to take lessons aren't allowed to wear sumptuous dresses and jewels, or unsuitable hairdos, or even perfume. They have to mortify themselves lest they unsettle us. It's a masquerade in reverse, of course. Obtained by subtraction rather than addition. And yet the rich girls still come to the Ospedale. In the evening it gets talked about, girl to girl. Let's also say that we give free vent to envy. One girl will have noticed that a pupil had dyed hair. Another will have spotted her well-trimmed nails. My companions cling to those details, it's as if they were looking through the chink of a lock of dyed hair or the tapered tip of a finger, through a keyhole, fantasising another life.

A lock of scorching hair, a filed nail. They are visions that hurt the girls of the Ospedale, they leave them bruised, injured.

I don't let these things fascinate me. I'm not afraid of the smuggled fashions that come into the Ospedale in dribs and drabs through the striking clothes worn by the daughters of the rich. What makes me anxious is the words they bring in here.

Lady Mother, in class, the teacher, the violinist Lucrezia, told the rich girl to put more intensity into it.
  'More what?' the girl asked.
  'Intensity, intensity.'
  'What's intensity?'
  'Force.'

'So I have to push more with my arm?'

'No, it's…'

'What?'

Lucrezia exploded: 'It's a force, yes, but also a force of feeling, not only of the muscles!'

'More passion, you mean?' asked the aristocratic girl.

'What?'

'Passion.' The girl's eyes had lit up. 'That feeling of being dragged forcefully towards someone you feel you love, when a person lights up your soul and everything within you is thrown into turmoil when you're close to them, and a happy pandemonium makes you…'

'Enough, enough, this isn't a lesson in grammar,' Lucrezia broke in. 'We need precise terms to achieve the best musical results, our purpose is not to plumb the specious subtleties of vocabulary.'

At this point there were some questions I would have liked to ask. I had never before heard the words turmoil and pandemonium. But above all I had never heard anyone use passion in that way. The passion is that of our Lord, who climbed the mountain to be tortured and killed, I knew that, his pain had to be vanquished bit by bit. Turmoil, pandemonium, passion… 'The things that happen near a person you love,' the rich girl had said.

The girls bring new words in here, or else they utter words already known to us, but with meanings that we hadn't heard used before. They are richer than us, not least because they experience more things and know what to call them, they know of the existence of many experiences of which we here at the Ospedale know nothing about.

I think again of how Lucrezia, the violin teacher, cut her off. 'We are not here to study grammar.' As if it were an evil.

Perhaps the evil is vocabulary. Now that I know you can feel turmoil, and pandemonium, and passion for a person you love... I know it even if I don't understand it... That rich girl sowed expectations within me. All the words in existence give rise to expectations.

So many things I feel within myself that I don't recognise because I don't know what to call them! And so many things I couldn't feel if I didn't possess their names. I remember the effect that the list of deadly sins had on me as a child. Envy was a word that made me discover so many things that happened within my soul, and in the attitudes of my companions here at the Ospedale. But sometimes I wonder if I wouldn't live better if I knew fewer words. In here I can't experience them to the full. I lead an abstracted life. Words spin around my head like flies. They buzz, I can't catch them, and when I do they're dead, I don't know what kind of life they led in other people's mouths, what they really mean.

Words are empty shells that a mollusc once lived in, but I don't know what they're like inside.

Words are warnings from the dead about things that exist.

Words are the revenge of the dead who fill them with wishes and expectations that are bigger than us.

Returning from a boat-trip, turning into a canal, we noticed that the water was changing colour. We looked at the sky, but there were no clouds above us, the sky was blue. From dark green, the water had turned yellowish, then brown, dark red.

'What is it?' we asked, disturbed.

'It looks like blood.'

'So much?'

The boat was soaking in a big dense vein.

'Do you think you could fill such a big canal with blood?

'And what's that stench?'

'It's blood, it is!'

'Look over there.'

'It's the slaughterhouse, the slaughterhouse of the animals!'

The cardinal's coming to hear us tomorrow. He's the head of the governors of the Ospedale. We'll have to look our best. We always have to look our best. Be in our places, fit in with the surroundings assigned to us.

He's written a concerto in which we all play. Mandolins, violas, flutes, oboes, lutes: even the little girls who only learned how to pick up a cello a few months before, even they have a small part to play solo, just a few bars, but enough to put them on show for a few moments. It's a strange concerto, the music passes, we all have our turn, one at a time or in groups, it's like a capricious gust of wind that sends eddies rising from one corner, then without warning from the opposite side of the hall.

Lady Mother, I'm here paying you a visit tonight again.

I couldn't sleep, then I thought of the little cellists, who will be running through in their minds and with the movements of their fingers the few bars that they will have to play tomorrow before the cardinal and the governors of the Ospedale. Even they probably won't be able to get to sleep. Everyone has worries. Who am I to think that mine are more important than other people's?

During the private concert, before the cardinal and the governors of the Ospedale, I was sitting near the little cellists. They were immersed in waiting for their turn, waiting for the moment when the gust of music would pass through them too, with their hearts in their throats.

Don Antonio wanted me to be the one to play along with him the main part for two violins. We had practised it together so many times that I played it from memory. I didn't even feel as if I was playing, just thinking what I was doing with the violin.

The cardinal was very satisfied, the concert will be repeated tomorrow in the church, in public.

At the last moment, Don Antonio took the part for two

violins out of the public concert, replacing it with a solo that he will play. And yet I had played everything perfectly, without any wrong notes. I don't understand. What did I do wrong?

Tonight the whole Ospedale was woken by an explosion. We climbed down from our beds, screaming. We heard an explosion that was louder than the first, then another.

'What's happening?'

'The Turks!'

'What? Are they here?' the dismayed voices asked, as the first lamps were lit.

'We defeated them! The Greek Sea is ours again!'

'Come to the window, look! The city is celebrating!'

Our ships have won back the Greek islands. When it seemed that all was lost, a brave attack by our men routed the Turks. We will celebrate the victory with an oratorio.

Don Antonio wrote the oratorio in just a few days. If you ask me, he already had it in his drawer. He prepares music for every occasion, weddings, funerals, parties and mournings. I'm sure he does it in advance, without waiting for a specific request. He must have an archive in which he stores the types of music appropriate to every occasion. I imagine him building up his collection of scores and setting them aside: 'This one has a rhythm that makes you want to move your legs, you can't sit still when you listen to it, it makes you dance, I'll send it to an aristocrat for a palace ball... This one brings even the most indifferent, the most carefree of people to tears, it'll be ideal for the funeral of a hateful ruler... This makes even a feeble sovereign seem solemn, it would make anyone bow as he passes, a provincial squire with regal ambitions will buy it from me... This is an abyss dug in heaven, it increases the glory of God, I'll give it to a foreign bishop who will take it with him and disseminate it throughout Europe...'

He translates every mood into music, he makes people listen to them and people get carried away: they are thrilled, or else they're moved, they weep. They are stunned by the way Don Antonio has been able to grasp their feelings of happiness, or sadness. While all he has done is to sell them back the normal running of his spirit. Each day has its sorrow, but also its contentment. Don Antonio listens to them inside himself, transcribes them onto the stave, offers the clients his banal inner dramas, his passing moods. They take them as universal incursions of the soul, and pay him well.

We will sing the story of Judith who offers herself to the chief of the enemies to save her people, enters Holofernes' tent to grant him her love and instead cuts off his head.

We will be performing a blind opera. In our theatre of the ear, the singers will be wearing costumes made of voice. They will sing behind the grilles, they will be invisible, as always. In order to make the nature of the characters understood they will have nothing but the timbre of their song.

'You're not sleeping?'
    'Who are you?'
    'How did you find your way here?'
    'I ended up here by chance.'
    'Are you telling me the truth?'
    'I couldn't sleep. I never can.'
    'And you came here to get cold?'
    'It isn't cold. I lean against this wall, it must be a chimney pipe, it's always warm.'
    'So you know it well!'

'What do you want from me?'

'The same thing you do. Let's talk for a while. Feel less alone.'

'You scared me.'

'What have I done that does not suit you?'

'You aren't the woman with the snake hair!'

'What are you talking about!?'

'A… A friend… Or an enemy, perhaps.'

'I don't understand.'

'I couldn't say who it was, but it was a woman who appeared to me without warning, and whom I haven't seen for a while.'

'With snake hair?'

'Yes, she had black hair, twisting, it moved, it was alive…'

'And I scare you more than a monster like that?'

'I'd finally got used to her …'

'And not to me?'

'What are you doing here?'

'I ought to be asking you that. You're the one who shouldn't have access to this part of the building. And at this time of night!'

'What about you?'

'I can go in and out at any time. Only to certain parts

of the Ospedale, of course. That's why you'd be better off going back to your room.'

'No one will find us.'

'How can you be sure?'

'I've been coming here since I learned to walk.'

'At last you're beginning to tell the truth.'

'I didn't know who I could trust.'

'And what are you doing here?'

'What am I not doing, you mean?'

'I don't understand.'

'I come here rather than toss and turn in bed all night without being able to get to sleep.'

'You too?'

'I saw you saying the mass.'

'Me, saying the mass? When?'

'A year ago. You had just arrived at the Ospedale a few days before. You celebrated the service in the dark, on your own, it was still night, but then you fell ill.'

'Oh, what a performance that was!'

'What?'

'To win over the nuns. After that they treated me as their little chick. They showered me with attention. There's nothing more appropriate than giving a woman with no children the excuse to feel a bit like a mother.'

My singing companions are excited, they hope they will be chosen to impersonate the protagonists of the Judith oratorio. Don Antonio is making everyone rehearse so that he can choose the right ones. I can't get worked up about their bickering in rehearsal. They pretend not to be envious, but meanwhile they give low blows at each other. I don't blame them. I feel sorry for them.

Lady Mother, I have found out a terrible thing. Yesterday I was talking to Maddalena about the oratorio that we're preparing, we were discussing the story of Judith and Holofernes. There are women in this city who act like Judith, much worse than her, who sacrificed herself for the good of her people by going into the enemy captain's tent. There are those who sell themselves, for money, and from that sale they give birth to children who are not wanted, and those children are suffocated in the womb, killed with poison, pulled out with irons when they are still tiny worms, or finished off as soon as they are born, or...

Or abandoned at the Ospedale.

Am I one of those as well? Lady Mother, am I the daughter of a coin?

The Judith oratorio will be another piece of tomfoolery by Don Antonio. We have to pretend to be a whole army with our little orchestra, the singers will become warriors hungry for women. I look Anita in the face as I rehearse the part of Holofernes and restrain myself to keep from exploding with laughter as we accompany her on our instruments, Anita hasn't the faintest clue about a bloodthirsty captain who gets drunk every night on girls procured by his soldiers. She makes a grim face, she turns quite red, she's the caricature of evil.

Laughing at her, I know even less about evil. That's what I can't forgive you for, Lady Mother, not you or anyone else in this Ospedale who takes care of me with such kindness. You prevent me from knowing evil, so that I may choose not to commit it.

It isn't enough to pretend to be an army, swords, horses: Don Antonio wants to complicate things, he has brought in a new instrument, a wind instrument, he makes it duet with Judith. Marta, who is singing that part, isn't at all happy, she says the sound blurs her voice, it's hard to distinguish her singing. In fact I think the new instrument is much lovelier than her voice. I crave the day when instruments will replace our voices entirely, things will overwhelm us, sweeping away all this pointless vehemence, all this passion, this pain.

The oratorio has been performed. The audience were moved, the public was excited, the state is safe, the invader is banished. Through the story of Judith and Holofernes, the aristocrats and the priests, sitting in the warm, indulged in a war waged by others. Also present in church were the leader of our army, a German, and his officers, all men who actually fought the battle that we are celebrating with this performance. Who knows what they must have thought as they remembered the clamour of war while hearing our harmonious chords.

It has been arranged that the aristocrats will meet the singers face to face. They will be able to visit the girls, along with the governors and the cardinal. The girls are desperate. They know they're ugly. They're preparing to be humiliated. The old aristocrats, fathers and mothers all, will inspect them, with the excuse of considering them for their sons, they will look them in the face just to satisfy their curiosity, they will assess them as one might do with horses at the market, and once they are outside they will laugh at them.

The aristocrats have arrived, the merchandise has been bought. Irene, with her twisted nose, and Marta, with her pox-pitted face, will be married to two boys from the wealthiest families in the city. Caterina, the lame one, is also about to be betrothed.

'Are you happy?' I asked Caterina.

'I can't wait to get out of here.'

'But you won't be able to put on concerts anywhere. We won't be able to sing or play if we leave here. The law prohibits the girls of the Ospedale from pursuing a singing career.'

'For me it's enough to be allowed to leave.'

'You're not sad to be abandoning music?'

'I want to hear the sound of things without playing them. I want to leave here and make noise, just noise.'

And me? What would I do if someone came one day and said to me: 'I want you'? If in your place, Lady Mother, a man presented himself and took me with him?

'How can they possibly get married?'

'Doesn't it seem fair to you that they too should have a chance?'

'I can't understand how they can have been chosen. They're...'

'Ugly?'

'No, it's more that...'

'Have the courage to say it. You think they're ugly, and no one could possibly want them as wives for their sons.'

'Yes.'

'I could tell you that my music transfigured them and made them look very beautiful and desirable.'

'But...'

'But you and I know very well that it would be a lie. A beautiful lie, but...'

'But a lie.'

'You might say that I compose music in order to organise marriages for the girls, so...'

'So, in a sense...'

'I'm a pimp!' Don Antonio started laughing.

'That's not what I meant.'

'But you thought it.'

'You suggested it yourself.'

'You're right. But you have to bear in mind that they

have good manners, and that they can make their mark in society.'

'Like furnishings to be put on display.'

'Their lack of attractiveness and their humble origins guarantee that home is the right place for them...'

'But... what about the husbands? Will they be happy to marry girls like that?'

'Do you think they're all young and rich? They are married to old widowers, or to lesser sons.'

'Why, is there such a thing as lesser sons?'

'Do you think you just have to have parents to be loved?'

'I myself don't, but...'

'Being an orphan has spared you a lot of disenchantments.'

Lady Mother, so I have a secret at the moment. When I come here to find you, when I sit down on the top step of the stairs to write to you covertly, I know that Don Antonio could come and chat with me at any moment. By day, between ourselves, we pretend nothing's happening. Is there anything wrong with that? Is it inappropriate? I have no one to confide in, and I don't want to. You are my confidante, as always. You are my niche of silence into which I throw everything that doesn't give me peace.

'Why didn't you want me to play in concert with you?'
    'Because you're small.'
    'But at the rehearsals and in the private performances for the governors and the cardinal…'
    'You're too young…'
    'I don't know how to play as one is supposed to?'
    'No one can tell you how to do that.'
    'All right, then, I didn't want to be proud, but I thought…'
    'You're better than good, you have a marvellous talent.'
    'So?'
    'Maybe I envy you.'

Lady Mother, today Don Antonio brought a violin sonata with a very strange and discordant part. Pretending nothing was awry he asked one of us to attempt it. He chose me, as if at random.

    'Given that you always play out of tune, this should suit you down to the ground,' he told me with a smile.

Lady Mother, I think he wrote it for me, or at least with me in mind. I'm afraid of that. Is it right? Is it wrong?

The thought scares me. Maybe it's me who's too proud, and I'm deluding myself that a composer worshipped by the whole city is going to start writing for an orphan girl He's a priest, I know, but he's also a young man, he might feel an attraction for a girl. Even though he's ugly, with his wiry, copper-coloured hair and his big nose. There, as I write and think about his face, I grow tender, I feel like smiling, and that's not good. I shall confide in you that I have imagined what Don Antonio would be like dressed as an angel, I have wondered whether the feathers of his wings would be copper-coloured as well, and whether... This is serious, I am no longer mistress of my thoughts, they torment me with forbidden imaginings, I'm shocked at myself.

And what if I weren't the proud one, and Don Antonio really had written that sonata for me? The wrong note that he's put into it is exactly the same one I played when he examined us one by one, in those first days, listening with his back to us. In his composition, it's no longer a real wrong note, because the bass receives it, it's as if it were throwing its arms open wide and catching in flight someone who had fallen, preventing them from crashing to the ground and hurting themselves.

Lady Mother, Don Antonio no longer comes to find me at night, to talk to me on this step. Perhaps he has realised that we were doing something bad, or that if we'd been discovered they would have thought who knows what about us. Perhaps he doesn't come because he's written that violin sonata with me in mind, and he's expecting me to reply in some way. Or perhaps he's worked out that he's done something serious, too serious, and he's holding himself back, he doesn't want to play with fire, he's being careful not to feed our flame.

Lady Mother, I'm distressed. My monthly blood is late. I'm afraid I might be pregnant.

I know how I got that way. I performed the sonata that Don Antonio wrote with me in mind, and now the seed that he left in my heart is growing inside me along with his music.

I dream of giving birth to my excrement in the latrines, at night.

The newborn child opens its mouth for the first time and starts singing, I scream in terror.

'Cecilia, don't run away.'

'This is my place. I discovered it.'

'Don't go away. I have to tell you something.'

'I don't want to hear anything more from you.'

'I've noticed that at rehearsals you only pretend to pay attention to me.'

'I do what is asked of me. I carry out orders.'

'Of course, but you're doing it mechanically.'

'The day you're no longer happy with my...'

'Oh, enough of this bickering! Let's forget about pride. I was going to say that last night I didn't tell you how things really are. I'm not envious of you. The truth is that... I'm jealous.'

'Don Antonio! What are you saying! You're a priest.'

'Have no illusions, little one. I'm jealous of your talent as a musician. If I make it shine in public now, you'll find a suitor straight away, and I'll lose you. I won't have you as a musician anymore.'

'But I'm ugly.'

'What are you talking about? We've managed to place hideous little monsters much less fascinating than you.'

'Why are you talking to me like that?'

'Don't cry, I was joking.'

'Sensitivity isn't your forte.'

'That's true. But I know how to talk to a girl with character. That's why I want to be honest with you: you will go on playing my music for many years, from behind the grille, but if anyone asks for your hand in marriage, you will refuse. Otherwise I will never let you perform anything in public ever again.'

'And you suggest this in exchange for what?'

'In exchange for music. I will make you play the most intoxicating pieces, you will shake people's souls to their foundations, that point at which our self dissolves into something coinciding with the vibrations of the cosmos.'

'You express yourself like a poet, but what you're suggesting is harsh.'

'What am I suggesting?'

'A life in prison.'

'I will make your name famous.'

'My name counts for nothing.'

'It will count, if you play what I write for you.'

'My name isn't me. I can't swap my happiness for the happiness of my name. There's nothing in a name.'

'I agree with you. You're wiser than me... Or rather no. You're just as wise as I expected you to be.'

'I'm just trying to defend myself against you.'

'So your answer is no?'

Lady Mother, for many days I've been spying on Sister Teresa. I've discovered where she keeps the keys, when she uses them and for how long. I stole them for half an hour. I came down to the room where the registers are kept. I found the cabinet and my page and I did something.

Don Antonio wanted a tour to be organised for the musicians who have contributed to the success of the Judith and Holofernes oratorio.

There were twelve of us in the boat, Don Antonio, some musicians and singers, Sister Teresa. We didn't know where we were being sent, Don Antonio wanted to give us a surprise. Rather than heading to one of the islands, we went touring around the internal canals. After passing under a three-arched bridge, the water started to turn red. We pulled up at the point where the blood was thickest. The girls didn't know what to say.

'Don't be scared. Let's go in,' Don Antonio said to us, but he asked Sister Teresa to wait for us in the doorway.

Lady Mother, I can't describe what I saw. Apart from the Ospedale, the church, the banks glimpsed through the slits in the mask and some off-shore islands, no one has ever shown me this city, I know nothing of the world, why start with this horrible place? The animals screamed their terror. It isn't true that they don't know they are mortal. We humans let them know before we kill them, by the way we kill them. We want them to know, to share our fate. We humans give them death together with the awareness of death. There can be nothing crueller than that. We can't bear that there are those who die innocent. We can't be the only ones to bear the weight of the awareness of our own death.

I listened to the last sound emitted by the one who knows the knife is about to be plunged into his heart, I saw his last glance. I can tell you no more than that, my words are breaking.

'Look, look well,' the priest said to us.

'Why are you doing this to us, Don Antonio?' I asked.

'It's necessary.'

'I don't understand.'

'Trust me.'

Then he took me aside and brought me into a room. There was a fire lit in a stove, some men, two buckets. A lamb.

'Go to them,' Don Antonio said to me.

I went. They put a leather protector around my body, it was an apron that covered me from my neck to my feet. They handed me a knife.

'Take it,' the priest said.

I clutched the knife in my hand.

A man immobilised the lamb by gripping it between his knees, grabbed the animal's head and pulled it back. Its throat was exposed. The man gave me a nod.

'No,' I said.

'Yes,' said Don Antonio. His voice was close to me now, I turned around. I saw him for a moment, standing behind me.

His hand took my wrist, guiding the blade to the animal's throat.

'Come on,' said Don Antonio, 'you have to be the one to do it.'

I shut my eyes and cut the lamb's throat.

I felt the soft scrape of the blade, its keen friction, the skin yielded, the blade plunged gently in, running like a bow along the strings, the creature emitted a bleat, it wasn't how I would have wanted to sound, it wasn't like that.

'Open your eyes, look at it!'

I felt the hot gush on my hand. I drew it back as if I'd been burned with a hot iron.

Why did he do that to me? Why?

Lady Mother, I'm not coming to find you again, I'm not going to write to you anymore.

Lady Mother, I no longer go to church, at night, to perform the music in my mind to offer my inner compositions to the Mother of God. I avoid going to sit down in the dark at the top of the stairs.

I will avoid unpleasant encounters. You know who I mean. But I am also referring to you, Lady Mother, have no illusions, you too are an unpleasant encounter, the worst of all, because you never come.

At night I just stretch out on my bed.

I no longer have any defences against anxiety.

The woman with the snake hair came back. She's so

solicitous, she always arrives when she hears she's needed. Her black head no longer talks to me. She looks me in the eye, throws her mouth open and screams.

At rehearsals I no longer gaze at Don Antonio. I receive orders and I obey. The words addressed to me become actions, gestures, performances. What do you want from me? Do you want me to pray, to play, to eat? Here I am. How must I breathe? How must I think? You tell me, do it for me. Please uproot me from myself. I don't want to know anything more about me. Just take whatever you want, substitute yourself for me, make me become what you are. It would be the greatest act of pity, in an instant it would rid me of me and you.

'I checked your violins before you arrived, you must tell me when the strings are old.'

'We had got used to not checking them too often. To save money.'

'Some of them were worn out. I changed them for you myself.'

Don Antonio gave me my violin. There was a new gut string, the most high-pitched one.

'It's lamb, that lamb,' he whispered to me, looking me

in the eyes. 'You earned it with your own hands. Now you have the right to play.'

Lady Mother, I have spent a week that I find hard to tell you about. I only know that for seven days I didn't want to touch my violin, I didn't want to know anything about music anymore, I was silent and I didn't address a word to anyone, I no longer wanted to see him. The nuns were disconcerted, but not too much, they are used to my eccentricities by now, they know I'm not just being flighty. Sister Teresa did her best to be gentle with me, but her voice seemed to reach me from so far away that I couldn't make out what she was saying to me, although I could hear that it was said in a caressing tone.

Then, after a week, I picked up my instrument and I started to play. I started in the morning and I didn't stop.

Don Antonio ordered that I was to be left alone. At least that was what I was told, because I wasn't aware of anything. I've been told that I went on playing until the middle of the night, until I was overcome by fatigue. They tell me my face was terrifying, I was frightening, I was stern and I was weeping. Everyone who listened to my playing burst into tears, they asked who had died that I loved so much, where so much bitterness came from, what I was commemorating that was so painful and irreparable. That's what seems to have happened, according to what my companions told me, and Sister Teresa confirmed it, but I can't accept it.

Lady Mother, this is the last time that I shall write to you. I have escaped from the Ospedale. I dressed as a man and boarded a boat. I understood what you wanted to tell me with the drawing of the wind-rose. When you left me new-born in the alcove at the Ospedale, I was dressed in green, that little green dress represented your maternal shirt, the bag of your belly from which I emerged. So the direction you were pointing me in was the opposite one, the missing part of the wind-rose, the blue pointers of the rays, the sea, the sky. That's what I did. We are sailing towards the Greek islands. From the envelope in the register I took the token, the half-wind-rose that I stole from the Ospedale archive. I threw it in the sea that night, as a good omen, as a suggestion to the currents that they might align themselves in the right direction and bring us to the place where my destiny awaits me. I will do the same with this page, when I have finished writing to you.

I lean over the railing of the ship, this time the balustrade is wide open, there are no metal grilles in front of me. I'm doing something I've never tried in my life. I've blocked my ears, I am staring at the stars, with my face in the air. I'm not listening, I'm looking. There's no ceiling above my head. In the register I've replaced my token with a picture of the Mother of God. It is neither cut nor torn. The other half of the token doesn't exist, because it isn't a paper token, it's me in flesh and blood, all of me, finally returned to myself and bound for my own fate.

Note

The first 33 rpm record I was given as a child was *The Four Seasons*, in the performance by Claudio Scimone's Solisti Veneti. Today there are two hundred Vivaldi compact discs in my house. But there is something else that binds me to the Venetian composer and his orphan musicians, something that dates back to before my childhood and coincides with my own coming into the world.

In the sixties of the last century, the maternity section of the Civic Hospital of Venice was located in the Ospedale della Pietà. I was delivered in that building, I was born in the rooms of the ex-orphanage, where Vivaldi taught and conducted his pupils, composing for them an endless stream of concertos and pieces of sacred music.

For me this coincidence was a kind of warning from fate, a seal upon the origin of my fantasy, *my thinking through characters* different from me: you have two parents who loved you, you were brought up in a family, but you could have been alone and without anyone, try and imagine yourself abandoned. For a long time I wanted to pay a tribute to the music of my favourite composer and the melancholy fate of his pupils.

The Pietà was one of the four institutions of the Venetian republic in which little orphans were brought up, to give them an education, a trade and the chance to enter society, not solely through marriage but also by granting them permission to give private music lessons. Some of the girls were part of the musical staff of those institutions, attracting an audience, benefactors and donations for the support of the orphanages. Thanks to their exceptional performing skills, the musicians of the Pietà attracted listeners from all over Europe, particularly during the decades in which Don Antonio Vivaldi lent his peerless flair to the institution.

Listening to these pieces of music, we tend to forget that they were composed for female performers. The musicians of the Pietà played suspended at a height of several metres, behind a balustrade, half-hidden by metal grilles that allowed a glimpse of their silhouettes but did not permit their faces to be studied.

In recent years, both Italian and foreign story-tellers have dedicated historical novels to Vivaldi. Virgilio Boccardi, in *Vivaldi a Venezia* (Canova, 2003), ran through the life in a novelised biography. Peter Harris has written *El Enigma Vivaldi* in Spanish (Plaza & Janes, 2006; but for the Italian market the author has been renamed Pedro Mendoza, *L'enigma Vivaldi*, Mondadori, 2007): he has imagined a contemporary violinist-researcher, who finds an unpublished Vivaldi score at the Ospedale della Pietà, of all places. Barbara Quick, in *Vivaldi's Virgins* (HarperCollins, 2007), has written a kind of autobiography of Anna Maria Dal Violin, Vivaldi's most famous pupil, in which she minutely reconstructs the daily life of the Ospedale and inserts into the narration some letters written by the fourteen-year-old protagonist to her mother, a device similar to the one that I have used in giving a voice to my Cecilia. Tito Gilberto in *Vivaldi: notte e follia del Prete Rosso* (Todaro Editore, 2007), turned his attention to Vivaldi's last years, in particular his unfortunate journey to Vienna, where the Venetian composer met his death. They are books which, lest I be influenced by them, I have barely flicked through or not even opened before starting to write my own.

To find the tone of my *Stabat Mater* (which for a

time I had entitled *Cimento di madre e di buio* – *Ordeal of Mother and Darkness* – echoing the celebrated collection of Vivaldi concerti) I found it useful to reread *Post mortem* by Albert Caraco (*L'âge d'homme*, 1968; Adelphi, 1984). For the liberty they demonstrate in their re-elaboration of the events of the past I was encouraged by the historical novellas of Gert Hofmann, above all *The Parable of the Blind* (*Der Blindensturz*, Hermann Luchterhand Verlag, 1985; Minerva 1989). My book is full of clamorous anachronisms. I shall mention only a few: neither the splendid oratorio *Juditha triumphans* nor indeed the concerti of the *Four Seasons* were composed in the first years of Vivaldi's teaching at the Pietà, as my pages would give the reader to understand. The list of incongruities in *Stabat Mater* would be very long and scattered with serious falsifications. Let it merely be said that I am perfectly aware of them; I beg the indulgence of historians and admirers of Vivaldi. I have taken the liberty of fantasising on the basis of a historical suggestion, without caring too much for documentary verisimilitude. I would be happy if this little homage to Vivaldi of mine prompted some readers to seek to know more, reading the works of historians and musicologists who have devoted impassioned studies to the Venetian composer and his pupils. Below I list some of the titles that I have used. Of them all I should like to single out the exceptional investigation by Pier Giuseppe Gillio into the Venetian musical orphanages of the 18th century.

Per Giuseppe Gillio, *L'attività musicale negli ospedali di Venezia nel Settecento*, Oschki, 2006.

Federico Moro, *Venezia in guerra, le grandi battaglie della Serenissima*, Mazzanti editori, 2007.

Egidio Pozzi, *Antonio Vivaldi*, L'Epos, 2007.

Michael Talbot, *Vivaldi*, Dent, 1978.

Micky White, Giuseppe Ellero and Gastone Vio, *Catalogo del Piccolo museo della Pietà Antonio Vivaldi*, 2004.

Alvise Zorzi, *La Repubblica del Leone. Storia di Venezia*, Bompiani, 2001.

Some compositions by Vivaldi are named in this book. Of the countless versions of the *Four Seasons*, my favourite is the one by the Concerto Italiano conducted by Rinaldo Alessandrini (Opus III/Naïve, 2003). Of the splendid oratorio *Juditha triumphans* I have a weakness for the recording by Alessandro De Marchi (Opus III/Naïve, 2001). Among the less recognisable allusions, the movement that contains sufficient melodic freedom to allow the possibility of a wrong note might be the Largo of the Sonata for Violin and Basso Continuo, No. 1 in C major, RV3 (particularly the performance by Andrew Manze, on the record '*Manchester' Sonatas* by the Ensemble Romanesca, Harmonia Mundi, 2002). In her last, hallucinatory improvisation on the strings of the lamb whose throat she herself has cut, Cecilia might equally be playing the Largo that serves as a prelude to the Sonata in F minor No 10, op 2, RV 21, in the performance by Hans Liviabella and Marco Decimo, *Sonate a violin e violoncello vol. I – Opera II e opera V*, Arkadia, 1994.

I was about to yield to the temptation of compiling a list of my favourite Vivaldi recordings, punctiliously indicating the individual movements and corresponding tracks of the compact discs, but I decided to restrict myself to a dozen or so.

Some people maintain, in line with the most timeworn clichés about Venice and the 17th century, that Antonio Vivaldi is a frivolous composer. I fear that in the past similar prejudices have weighed upon attitudes to the performance of Vivaldi's music. As in literature and many other areas, there are certain authors and powerful works that can be undermined by people who don't take

them seriously. To put it whimsically, Vivaldi unfolds his
potential if you play him with a pinch of the reverence
reserved all too pompously for Bach. So my list includes
some of the interpreters and performers who have taken
Vivaldi's music seriously.

Concerti e Trii per liuto e archi, Massimo Lonardi, Conserto
    Vago, Paragon/Amadeus, 2002.
Concertos and Chamber Music, Musica Alta Ripa, MDG,
    1999.
Concertos pour violoncelle, vol. 1 and vol. 2, Roel Dieltiens,
    Ensemble Explorations, Harmonia Mundi, 1998 and
    2002.
Dixit Dominus, Francesco Fanna, Instituto Italiano
    Antonio Vivaldi, 2007.
Flute Concertos op X, Camerata Köln, Harmonia Mundi,
    1990.
Sinfonie 'Avanti l'Opera' – Concerti, Christopher
    Hogwood, L'Arte dell'Arco, 2002.
Six Concertos for Flute, Strings and B. c. op. 10, Konrad
    Hünteler, Camerata of the 18th century, MDG, 1996.
Sonatas for violoncello solo del signor Antonio Vivaldi, Bruno
    Cocset, Les Basses Réunies, Alpha, 1999.
Stabat mater, Sara Mingardo, Rinaldo Alessandrini,

Concerto Italiano, Opus III/Naïve 2002.

Vespri per l'Assunzione di Maria Vergine, Gemma Bertagnolli, Roberta Alessandrini, Concerto Italiano, Opus III/ Naïve, 2003.